Daughter
The Birth
and Ven

by Sumiko Nakano

© **Sumiko Nakano Ltd.**

Registered Office: 2nd Floor College House, 17 King Edwards Road, Ruislip, London, United Kingdom, HA4 7AE

All rights reserved. No part of this publication may be reproduced, stored in a retrieval system, distributed, or transmitted in any form or by any means—electronic, mechanical, photocopying, recording, or otherwise—without the prior written permission of the copyright holder, except in the case of brief quotations used in reviews, scholarly articles, or permitted by applicable copyright law.

For permissions, licensing inquiries, or other legal matters, please contact:

Sumiko Nakano Ltd., Attention: Permissions Coordinator
Email: **info@sumiko-nakano.com**

This work is protected by copyright under the laws of the United Kingdom and international copyright conventions.

Preface	2
Historical Note	5
Prologue	8
1: Echoes of the Past	11
2: The Art of War and Words	16
3: Signs of Turmoil	21
4: The Silence Broken	25
5: The Abduction	34
6: Captive Shadows	39
7: Night of the Vengeful Shadow	54
8: Dawn of Reunion And Resolve	85
Epilogue	91
Glossary	94
Preview: The Broken Oath	98

In the depth of winter, I finally learned that within me there lay an invincible summer." — Albert Camus

To the brave souls who weave the threads of their fates with the steel of their resolve.

Preface

In the swirling mists of a Japan caught between the rigid structures of the past and the pulsing promise of a new era, three sisters carve a path marked by courage, sorrow, and an unyielding commitment to each other. "Daughters of Wars: The Birth of Steel and Vengeance" is a tale of resilience in the face of overwhelming odds, a narrative that intertwines the personal battles of its characters with the larger tumult of historical upheaval.

The Hayashi sisters—Sumiko, Misako, and Aiko—embody the spirit of the onna-bugeisha, female warriors who rise beyond the conventional expectations of their time. Inspired by the legends of their ancestors and driven by a deep love for their family, they engage in a quest not just for survival, but for justice and honor.

This novel is not merely an exploration of historical events but a vivid portrayal of how the personal and the historical intersect in the lives of individuals. It is about the choices they make, the sacrifices they endure, and the unbreakable bonds that sustain them. Each sister, distinct in her own right, contributes to a collective strength that challenges the encroaching forces threatening their way of life.

As you embark on this journey with Sumiko, the silent lioness; Misako, the fiery spirit; and Aiko, the strategic intellect, I invite you to witness not just a series of battles fought with blades, but also conflicts waged in the hearts and minds of these formidable women.

In these pages, the past is not merely recounted; it is relived. The echoes of clashing swords, the whispers of strategy, and the quiet moments of sisterly love are as vivid as if painted on silk. Herein lies an invitation to lose yourself in a story of a family, a legacy, and a fight for honor that transcends the boundaries of time.

Welcome to the world of the Hayashi sisters, where every strike is a word, every defense a line, and every victory a chapter in the grand narrative of their lives.

DAUGHTERS OF WARS

Beneath the moon's watchful gaze,
Three spirits dance in storm's embrace.
The silent stream, deep and steadfast,
A fiery blaze, fierce and vast.
Gentle breeze, wise and unseen,
In the garden of stones, their essence keen.

Rooted deep in sacred ground,
Through shadows' grasp, their strength is found.
Together they rise, their courage bright,
As stars that guide through the darkest night.

Historical Note

By late 1867, Japan stood on the threshold of collapse. For more than two centuries, under the Tokugawa shogunate, the country had embraced a policy of national seclusion—sakoku—rejecting foreign contact and preserving a strict social order under samurai rule. That era was ending.

In 1853, American warships under Commodore Matthew Perry entered Edo Bay, demanding that Japan open its ports to the outside world. What followed was a series of unequal treaties, signed under pressure, that dismantled the foundations of Japan's isolation. Foreign merchants, diplomats, and military observers flooded into cities once closed to outsiders. Steam power, firearms, and Western dress appeared in markets still echoing with the sounds of geta on stone.

The old balance fractured. Power that once resided in the shogunate began to slip—first quietly, then violently. The emperor, long a figurehead in Kyoto, was reasserted by reformist factions as a rallying symbol for national unity and renewal. Loyalist samurai, court nobles, and ambitious domain lords began to speak not of loyalty to the Tokugawa but of restoration. In truth, it was revolution.

The social order that had defined Japan for centuries—samurai, peasants, artisans, merchants—was cracking. The samurai, once the unquestioned elite, now found their status uncertain. Many were left unpaid. Others were rearmed, radicalized, or cast aside. Some aligned with the old regime. Others defected. The codes of bushidō still lingered in their blood—but what those codes meant in a world reshaping itself with steel, steam, and foreign ideas was a question no one could answer.

Domains such as Aizu, Satsuma, Chōshū, and Tosa became major players in a volatile political game. Aizu remained among the most loyal to the Tokugawa, upholding strict military discipline and Confucian governance even as other regions turned against the old order. Internal rivalries between these domains—masked as ideology—escalated into violence in the streets of Kyoto. Assassinations became common. Secret factions gathered support under the banner of imperial restoration.

In November 1867, Tokugawa Yoshinobu, the fifteenth and final shogun, officially resigned and returned power to the Emperor. On the surface, this act seemed to promise a peaceful transition. In truth, it was a tactical move—and the spark for war. Imperial forces began to consolidate. Loyalist and Tokugawa factions prepared for battle. Japan's unity was an illusion waiting to be shattered.

The war that followed—known as the Boshin War—would

break out in January 1868. It marked not just the end of the shogunate but the violent birth of a new Japan. The Meiji Restoration, as it would later be called, swept away centuries of feudalism. The samurai were dissolved as a class. The imperial court was modernized. Western law, military systems, and education began to reshape the nation. And with each reform, the echoes of the old world grew quieter.

This book series in the final days before that collapse. A moment in time when the storm had not yet broken, but the sky was already cracked. When ancient loyalties still held—but barely. When the roads were watched, the swords were drawn, and the empire still pretended it could survive without consequence.

What came next would decide everything.

...

Prologue

In the final winter of the Tokugawa shogunate, Japan held its breath—and the silence was not peace. It was something colder. Something splintering.

Edo still called itself the center of power, but no one was listening. The Shogun had stepped down. The Emperor had stepped forward. And now, every man with a sword was choosing who to die for. Lords whispered of loyalty while watching their neighbors more than their enemies. Allies bowed with smiles too careful. Orders came late. Promises came hollow. And the weight of something unspoken pressed down on every corner of the land.

By late 1867, the maps were still the same, but nothing else was. What held the country together was not strength, but memory—and even that was starting to fade.

Far from the cities where power shifted hands in silence, beyond the corridors of Kyoto and Edo, a village sat buried in the folds of a forested ridge beneath Aizu's reach. No banners flew above it. No festivals announced the seasons. But everyone knew which way to bow. And which names not to speak.

In that village, just before dawn, three sisters moved through the snow.

Sumiko moved like she'd been carved from stillness. Her silence wasn't absence—it was weight. Misako, all fury and instinct, struck like fire in a world too slow to keep up. And Aiko, youngest, moved just behind them, watching everything. Her mind was sharper than her blade. And her blade was already sharp enough to kill.

They were not girls anymore. But they had not yet become what the world would force them to be.

Their father trained them. He did not flatter. He did not explain. He commanded. His presence carried more discipline than warmth, and the air in the house bent around him like heat over a forge. He had served Aizu his whole life. That much the village believed. The rest was speculation and silence.

Whatever his past was, it moved with him—like a shadow a little too close, a little too heavy. Letters arrived without return seals. Strangers came asking the wrong kind of questions. And though he said nothing, he had begun watching the ridgeline with a hunter's stillness, like he was waiting for something to crest it.

The sisters didn't ask. They only trained harder.

January brought no snowmelt. The ground stayed frozen. Travel slowed. Conversations shifted. There was a taste to the air like iron, like blood not yet spilled. And still the empire pretended.

But the sisters didn't.

They woke before sunrise. They drilled. They moved like they were already being watched. Because maybe, they were.

The war had not yet begun.

But the dying had.

And the Hayashi sisters were no longer waiting.

•••

1: Echoes of the Past

The morning mist shrouded the quaint village Kasumigaura nestled beneath the somber peaks of northern Honshu, a silent witness to the ancient rites of a world fading into the echoes of history. Here, among the whispering pines and thatched roofs soaked with dew, lived the Hayashi sisters—Sumiko, Misako, and Aiko—trained in the ways of the warrior by their father, a samurai whose honor was as renowned as his skill with the blade.

As dawn broke, casting its first golden rays over the landscape, the sounds of wooden staves and steel clashing filled the air from the family dojo. Sumiko, the eldest at 25, moved with a serene grace, her naginata slicing through the morning air. Misako, fierce and impulsive at 21, swung her katana with a wild energy that mirrored the fire in her spirit. Aiko, young and clever at 18, practiced her strokes, her form still unrefined but promising.

Their father watched from the side, his gaze heavy with thought. "Very good," he finally spoke, his voice echoing slightly in the spacious dojo. "But remember, true strength comes not from the sword alone, but from the spirit within."

Sumiko nodded silently, her face calm but her eyes reflecting a depth of unspoken thoughts. She hadn't spoken a word since the age of nine, when a devastating fire claimed their mother's life and stole her voice. That day had marked them all, but for Sumiko, it had carved a silence that she wore like an invisible mantle.

Misako sheathed her sword with a flourish, her brow furrowing. "I understand, father, but how can we prepare for what's coming? Rumors of war are spreading like wildfire. If it reaches our village—"

Aiko, ever the voice of reason, interjected, signing swiftly as she spoke, translating Sumiko's gestures. "Misako worries about the unrest, father. We all do. How did our ancestors face such times?"

Their father's eyes softened as he sat down, gesturing for them to join him. "With courage and wisdom," he began, his voice a low rumble. "Our ancestors stood firm in times of chaos, guided by Bushido. We must do the same, even if the storm descends upon us."

Sumiko signed, her hands moving with a fluid grace, and Aiko translated, "But how did they keep their hearts strong in the face of fear?"

"They found strength in each other and in their duty," he replied, looking between his daughters. "As you must do. Sumiko, your strength is in your calm, your ability to lead without words. Misako, your fiery spirit can spark courage in others. And Aiko, your cleverness will be our guide."

As they absorbed their father's words, a distant memory surfaced—the sound of their mother's laughter, the warmth of her embrace, and the night that had stolen it all away. The fire had started so quickly, engulfing their home with merciless fury. Sumiko, only a child then, had tried to save her mother, rushing into the flames. But it was too late, and the fire had cruelly taken her voice, leaving her in a silence that had never since been broken.

The sisters exchanged glances, each carrying their own pain from that night, but also a shared resolve. They returned to their positions, their movements now infused with a renewed purpose. As they trained, the sun climbed higher, and the village stirred to life, oblivious to the quiet determination growing in the heart of the dojo.

Their father's voice followed them as they practiced, "Remember, the strength of a samurai lies not just in the skill of arms but in the courage to face whatever comes with honor and resolve."

...

The day moved forward, but the past lingered in the air, a constant reminder of what had been lost and what could still be lost.

As the morning session in the dojo drew to a close, the Hayashi sisters settled into a quiet moment of reflection, their breathing still heavy from the exertion. The dojo, filled with the soft clatter of wooden beams cooling in the morning air, held within its walls the echoes of their rigorous training and the deep bonds they shared as sisters and warriors.

Sumiko, the eldest, sat slightly apart, her gaze fixed on the distant mountains visible through the open door. In her silence, there was a profound strength and a palpable sense of leadership. Despite, or perhaps because of, her inability to speak, she communicated with a clarity that transcended words. Her movements were deliberate and thoughtful, whether in battle or in daily interactions. The loss of her voice had deepened her inner life, making her expressions and gestures rich with meaning. She had become adept at using sign language, which Aiko often translated, but those who knew her well understood much from her eyes and demeanor alone. To her sisters, Sumiko was more than just a sibling; she was a beacon of stability and a quiet powerhouse whose presence alone could reassure and inspire.

Misako was the fire to Sumiko's calm waters. With her vibrant energy and impulsive nature, she often acted as the spark that set their plans into motion. Her emotions played freely across her features, from fierce determination in battle to warm laughter during quieter moments. Misako's spirited approach to life brought lightness to their often serious existence, but it also meant she sometimes clashed with the more measured strategies Sumiko preferred. Yet, beneath her fiery exterior lay a deep loyalty to her family and a courage that made her a formidable warrior. She was often the first to challenge injustice or leap to the defense of those in need, driven by a passionate heart that refused to back down.

Aiko, the youngest, carried a quiet intelligence and an observant nature that complemented her more outspoken sisters. Her cleverness was not just in strategy or learning but in understanding people, a skill that made her an invaluable mediator within their trio. Aiko's role often involved interpreting Sumiko's signs and ensuring that Misako's enthusiasm didn't lead them astray.

Her thoughtful presence brought balance to their group, grounding them with her rational perspective and insightful observations. Aiko also harbored a profound sense of duty, perhaps more academic and reflective, shaped by the many hours she spent poring over texts and practicing calligraphy, absorbing the lessons of the past to navigate their future.

As they each sat contemplating their father's teachings, the bond among them was palpable, a silent yet powerful affirmation of their unity and shared purpose. They were each distinct in their way, but together, they formed a formidable force, ready to face the changes stirring beyond their village.

The dojo's peacefulness was a stark contrast to the challenges they knew lay ahead. As they rose to continue their day, the connection between them was a silent vow to protect each other and their home, whatever the cost. With each sister embodying a unique aspect of the warrior spirit—calm, fire, and wisdom—they were not just survivors of past tragedies but shapers of their own destinies, guided by the unwavering principles of Bushido that had been passed down through generations.

•••

2: The Art of War and Words

In the cool shade of the early morning, the Hayashi dojo came alive with the sounds of earnest preparation. Each sister delved into her training with a dedication that spoke volumes of their upbringing under their father's vigilant eye. This morning was particularly intense, as their father decided it was time to deepen their understanding of the martial and intellectual disciplines that shaped a true warrior.

Sumiko stood poised with her naginata, the staff weapon that had become an extension of her own spirit. Her movements were fluid and controlled, a dance of precision that melded strength with elegance. Even without her voice, she commanded attention, her silent instructions as clear as any spoken command. She paired with Aiko, guiding her through complex maneuvers, correcting her stance with a gentle touch and a firm sign.

Misako, on the other hand, engaged in a more aggressive sparring session with one of the dojo's senior students. Her katana flashed in the sunlight, each stroke delivered with a raw power that her opponent found difficult to counter. "Control,

Misako! Remember, the blade is as much about finesse as it is about force," their father admonished from the sidelines.

Their father, once satisfied with the physical routines, gathered them for the day's lesson on strategy and philosophy. They sat in a semi-circle around him, each sister with her weapon resting beside her. "Today, we delve into the works of Sun Tzu and Musashi," he announced, unrolling a scroll with ancient text. "Understanding strategy will guide you in combat and life.

He read aloud a passage, his voice resonant in the quiet morning, "All warfare is based on deception. Thus, when we are able to attack, we must seem unable; when using our forces, we must appear inactive; when we are near, we must make the enemy believe we are far away; when far away, we must make him believe we are near."

Aiko, quick to grasp the underlying meanings, signed a question for Sumiko to translate, "Father, how do we apply these teachings directly in battle?"

Their father smiled, pleased with her inquisitiveness. "Good question, Aiko. In battle, positioning and the element of surprise can turn the tide. For example, feigning weakness can draw the enemy into a trap where you have the advantage. It's not just about physical confrontation but outthinking your opponent."

As the lesson continued, they discussed the philosophical aspects of Musashi's "The Book of Five Rings," focusing on the concept of 'void'—the idea of knowing what is not there as much as what is. "To master the void is to be fluid, adaptable in your thoughts and actions," their father explained.

Sumiko signed her thoughts, which Aiko translated, "It's like being water, adapting to the form of whatever contains it but always retaining its essence."

"Yes, exactly," their father nodded, visibly proud. "Being adaptable in combat and life is crucial. You must be fluid like water, strong like the earth, swift as the wind, and as consuming as fire."

As the sisters gathered around their father in the dojo's serene environment, the air was thick with the anticipation of a deeper dive into the Bushido code, the very essence of their training and life philosophy.

Their father began, his voice carrying the weight of tradition and wisdom. "Now, let us discuss the heart of Bushido—the way of the warrior. It's more than skill and technique; it's a way of life. It embodies virtues that you must carry not just in battle but in every aspect of your existence."

Misako, ever the most outspoken, leaned forward, her eyes bright with curiosity. "Father, you speak of virtues. We know of honor and courage, but how do these apply when the choices are not clear, when the path forward is shrouded in shades of moral ambiguity?"

Their father nodded appreciatively at her question. "Honor and courage are fundamental, yes. But consider also rectitude, or justice. Making the right decision, especially when the path is not clear, is the true test of a samurai. You must weigh your actions not only against your survival but against what is righteous, for our actions echo beyond the battlefield."

Sumiko, her presence as calm and commanding as ever, signed a question, her movements graceful yet imbued with intent. Aiko, interpreting for her, relayed, "Sumiko asks about benevolence. How do we maintain compassion in a path marked by conflict?" Their father's eyes softened, "Benevolence, or jin, is what distinguishes a true warrior from a mere fighter. Despite the violence we may encounter, we must never lose our capacity for compassion towards the innocent and those who depend upon us. This is the strength that sustains a community, that builds a legacy worth defending."

Aiko, who had been quietly absorbing every word, finally spoke, her voice thoughtful. "And what of loyalty? How do we balance our loyalty to our superiors with the loyalty we owe to ourselves, to our own moral compass?"

Their father smiled, proud of her insight. "Loyalty is indeed complex. True loyalty involves questioning, understanding, and sometimes, standing against wrongful orders. It is not blind obedience but a dedication to the greater good, to the principles that underlie Bushido itself."

As the conversation deepened, they explored the nuances of honor, the virtue perhaps most synonymous with Bushido. "Honor is not about pride or personal glory," their father explained. "It is about living in such a way that one's actions reflect well not only on oneself but also on one's family and one's ancestors. It is the invisible thread that connects our actions to our heritage."

The dialogue then shifted to practical applications, discussing historical battles and legendary samurai who exemplified these virtues. They dissected decisions made in the heat of combat, exploring how each decision reflected the principles of Bushido. As the shadows lengthened and the dojo grew quiet, the sisters sat in deep reflection. This discussion had not only illuminated the complexities of the Bushido code but had also tied them more closely to the path they had chosen—or perhaps, the path that had chosen them.

Their father concluded, "Remember, the strength of Bushido lies within, in making decisions that align with these virtues, no matter the external pressures. As you grow in skill, so too must you grow in wisdom."

•••

3: Signs of Turmoil

The tranquility of Kasumigaura, home to the Hayashi family, was slowly overshadowed by distant murmurs of unrest as political winds shifted across Japan. With the Tokugawa shogunate's grip weakening and imperial ambitions strengthening, the nation stood on the brink of a profound transformation. In the midst of these rumblings, the Hayashi dojo remained a steadfast haven of discipline and learning, but even here, the echoes of change were palpable.

On a crisp morning, the villagers gathered for a regional meeting, convened by none other than the sisters' father, who was not only their sensei but also the village headman. He stood before his fellow villagers, a figure of resolve clad in traditional samurai garb, his voice steady and commanding.

"Times are changing," he began, his gaze sweeping over the crowd of familiar faces, "and we must be ready to stand for our beliefs and protect our way of life. Loyalty to our lord and to each other will guide us through whatever may come."

Sumiko, Misako, and Aiko stood by his side, each embodying

the virtues he preached. Sumiko's calm demeanor belied the strategic mind that had absorbed countless lessons on warfare and leadership. Misako's fiery spirit seemed to spark with readiness, her hand resting lightly on the hilt of her katana. Aiko, with a thoughtful frown, translated Sumiko's silent signs for the villagers, who knew and respected the sisters' unique bond.

The meeting addressed the practicalities of defense—how to fortify the village, the training of the militia, and the stockpiling of supplies. Misako spoke passionately about the need for rigorous combat readiness, drawing nods and murmurs of agreement. "We are not just defending land," she declared, "we are defending our homes, our families, and our freedoms!"

As the discussions unfolded, Aiko found herself mingling with the villagers, sharing insights and listening to their concerns. Her intelligence and warmth drew people to her, and she relayed these interactions to Sumiko, whose silent observations often caught details others missed.

Their father concluded the meeting with a call to unity. "This village is not just a place on a map," he asserted. "It is a community, a family. We stand together, or we fall divided."

Later, as the sisters walked back to their home, they discussed the weight of their father's words. "Do you think war will truly come to us?" Aiko asked, a hint of worry in her voice.

Sumiko signed her response, which Aiko translated for Misako, "War affects everyone, no matter how distant it seems. We must be prepared, not just physically but mentally."

Misako clenched her fists, her resolve hardening. "Let them come. We will show them the strength of the Hayashi."

As the sisters continued their walk, the evening air crisp and the path beneath their feet covered with fallen leaves, they delved deeper into their concerns and strategies.

Aiko, always the one to seek understanding, broke the silence that had settled after Misako's bold declaration. "It's not just about fighting," she said thoughtfully. "It's about what we're fighting for. Father spoke of loyalty and unity, but how do we ensure everyone in the village feels the same way?

How do we maintain morale if the war does reach our doorstep?"

Sumiko stopped walking, her expression serious as she signed her response, her movements deliberate and clear. Misako watched her carefully, then translated for Aiko. "Sumiko believes that morale is maintained not just through strength of arms but through strength of spirit. She suggests regular gatherings, not just meetings for defense planning, but also for sharing stories, celebrating our culture, and remembering our history. It's the spirit of the community that will sustain us through the hardest times."

Misako nodded, her earlier fire now tempered with contemplation. "That's a wise approach. And it's proactive. We should start these gatherings soon, make them a regular part of village life before any crisis hits. It will bind us together and remind everyone what we're fighting to protect."

Aiko smiled, pleased with the suggestion. "I could organize

storytelling evenings. We could use tales of our ancestors, the great battles they fought, and the values they upheld. It would be educational but also inspiring."

The idea seemed to energize them both, and even Sumiko, typically reserved, showed a flicker of approval in her eyes. She signed again, and Misako translated. "Sumiko also suggests involving the children more actively in our traditions. Perhaps training sessions for the younger ones, not just in martial arts but in other aspects of our samurai heritage."

"That's brilliant," Aiko agreed. "Engaging the children will ensure our traditions continue, no matter what comes. And it will give their parents comfort to see them strong and capable."

As they neared their home, the light from the windows casting warm glows onto the path, the sisters felt a renewed sense of purpose. They had tasks to accomplish, plans to implement, and a village to prepare. They were not just defenders with blades but keepers of a way of life, a role they now embraced more fully than ever. Inside, they gathered around a small table, maps and scrolls spread out before them. They plotted, planned, and prepared, each sister contributing her unique strengths to the discussion. Their father joined them, listening intently, occasionally offering guidance or a nod of approval.

"The challenges ahead are daunting," he acknowledged, "but with your minds and hearts committed to our cause, I have no doubt that Kasumigaura will not only endure but emerge stronger. You three are the heart of this village, and your unity is its strength."

The evening wore on, filled with discussions of logistics and legacies.

4: The Silence Broken

As the seasons shifted, so did the atmosphere in the Hayashi village. What had once been silence was now tension—subtle at first, then unmistakable. The rumble of conflict no longer felt distant. Whispers of political fractures and shifting allegiances reached even this remote place, carried on the wind like warnings. The war had not yet begun—but its shadow was already at their doorstep.

In response, the Hayashi dojo became a hub of heightened activity. Sumiko took charge of the strategic preparations, organizing patrols and overseeing the fortifications of the village. Her silent authority brought calm to the chaos, her signs and gestures translating into commands as clearly as any spoken word.

Misako, fueled by her fiery spirit, trained the villagers with a relentless intensity. Her sessions were grueling but effective, turning even the most inexperienced villagers into capable fighters. "Your will is your weapon," she would shout over the clatter of wooden swords. "Your courage, your shield!"

Aiko, meanwhile, focused on gathering intelligence. She moved through the village and the surrounding areas, her keen mind piecing together snippets of information into a larger strategic picture. She was also responsible for communication, using her skills in sign language to relay messages between Sumiko and the rest of the team.

•••

As the Hayashi sisters convened in the warmth of their home, preparing for what seemed an inevitable confrontation, their father's absence was notably palpable. Typically the anchor in their discussions of defense and strategy, his chair stood empty, a silent testament to the responsibilities that had called him away. Earlier in the week, their father had been summoned to Aizu Castle—a significant event given the volatile political climate. The purpose of the meeting was to strategize with other samurai leaders from the region. As the Tokugawa shogunate's power waned, those loyal to the old ways sought to forge alliances and plan defenses against the encroaching forces of the Emperor, who were intent on consolidating power and enforcing the new imperial rule.

Their father, known for his strategic acumen and deep commitment to the samurai code, was a vital participant in these discussions. He was expected to lend his expertise in both martial and ethical matters, helping to shape a response that balanced fierce resistance with the honorable conduct befitting a samurai.

"This meeting at Aizu Castle is critical," he had explained before his departure. "We are not just planning for battle but for the preservation of our way of life. I must be there, to ensure our voices are heard, and our strategies are sound."

With their father at this crucial assembly, the burden of immediate decision- making fell squarely on the sisters' shoulders, a challenge they accepted with a mix of trepidation and resolve. His absence, while keenly felt, served as a stark reminder of the leadership roles they were increasingly required to assume.

One evening, as the sisters discussed their plans in the quiet of their home, a frantic knock shattered the calm. A village scout, breathless and pale, brought word: a group of armed men had been spotted approaching—some clad in imperial uniforms, others dressed as ronin. It wasn't a formal army, but it moved like it had orders. And it was coming straight for Kasumigaura.

"Their numbers are great, and they move fast," he reported, his voice trembling with urgency. "They could be here by dawn."

Now, as they faced the news of the advancing imperial soldiers, their father's teachings echoed in their minds—his lessons on courage, strategy, and unity. It was these principles that would guide them through the storm that was fast approaching their village.

"We'll implement the defense plans father helped us prepare," Misako stated firmly, her hand unconsciously gripping the hilt of her katana as if drawing strength from its familiar feel.

Aiko nodded, her expression composed as she added, "I'll coordinate the villagers, ensure everyone knows their role. We can use the signal fires to alert the outlying farms."

Sumiko, her presence a calming force, signed her instructions, which Aiko quickly translated for the benefit of the scout, "Tell everyone to be ready. We fight not just for Kasumigaura but for each other."

As the scout hurried away to spread the word, the sisters prepared for the night ahead. They fortified entry points, checked on their stockpiles of weapons, and conferred with the village's makeshift militia. Though their father's presence was missed, his teachings were their guide, his spirit their inspiration. The night grew deeper, the tension palpable in the cool air. But within the walls of the Hayashi home, the resolve of three sisters, trained by a samurai of the old guard, burned brighter than any fear the approaching dawn might bring.

The sisters exchanged a quick glance, each understanding the gravity of the situation. Sumiko's face was a mask of resolve, Misako's eyes blazed with a fierce determination, and Aiko's expression was set in a grim line.

"We will meet them head-on," Sumiko signed, her hands steady. Aiko quickly translated, "We will defend our home, no matter the odds."

That night, under Sumiko's leadership, the village transformed into a fortress. Barricades rose, traps were set, and every able-bodied man and woman was armed and positioned. Misako walked among them, her presence a rallying force, instilling courage with every fiery word she spoke.

Aiko coordinated the scouts and messengers, ensuring that communication lines remained open and effective. Her ability to synthesize information quickly was crucial as they adjusted their defenses based on the movements of the imperial troops.

As the first light of dawn tinged the sky with gray, the distant sound of marching feet became audible. The village held its breath, waiting for the battle to begin. The Hayashi sisters stood together at the front line, their faces resolute, their weapons ready.

The initial clash was violent and sudden. Imperial soldiers surged over the rise like a flood, their armor gleaming under the rising sun, their shouts filling the air. The villagers, bolstered by the sisters' leadership, met the charge with a fierce cry of their own, their makeshift weapons clashing against the polished steel of the imperial forces.

Sumiko was the first to engage. Her naginata sliced through the air, its blade whistling a deadly tune. She moved with a dancer's grace, each step and turn calculated and precise. Her opponents underestimated her due to her silence, a mistake that cost them dearly as she disarmed one soldier after another, her movements a blend of art and deadly efficiency.

Misako, filled with a raging fire, fought like a tempest. Her katana was an extension of her will, cutting down enemy after enemy in sweeping arcs. She roared challenges at the imperial soldiers, drawing them towards her, her blade a blur of motion. Despite her ferocity, the strain of battle was evident on her face, sweat mixing with the dirt and blood spatter, her breath coming in harsh gasps as she fought tirelessly.

Aiko, less experienced in direct combat, used her intelligence and agility to compensate for her lack of brute strength. From higher ground, she loosed arrows with calm precision, picking off threats before they reached the village. Her bow was not just a weapon—it was strategy in motion. Between volleys, she repositioned with quiet speed, always scanning the battlefield, adjusting her aim at the slightest signal from Sumiko. She didn't fight to overpower. She fought to outthink—and every arrow flew exactly where it needed to land.

The battle raged on, neither side yielding. The ground became muddy with blood and trampled earth, the air thick with the cries of the wounded and the dying. It was a brutal, merciless fight, and though the sisters were skilled, they were not invincible. Each felt fear gripping their hearts as they witnessed the devastation around them, their bodies aching, their spirits tested to the limits.

Sumiko received a shallow cut on her arm, a stark reminder that she too was vulnerable. Misako helped a young villager to his feet, only to see him fall again, a spear piercing his chest. Aiko felt a moment of panic as an enemy soldier nearly broke through her guard, his blade grazing her shoulder.

Yet, amidst this chaos, the bond between the sisters proved to be their greatest strength. They fought back-to-back at times, covering each other's weaknesses, their combined force greater than the sum of its parts. They shouted words of encouragement, rallied their fellow villagers, and fought not just for survival, but for the very soul of their village.

As the sun climbed higher, the battle intensified. Every strike, every block, every moment of fear and triumph was a testament to their training, their father's teachings, and their unyielding spirit. The Hayashi sisters, through blood, sweat, and tears, were not just fighting—they were defending a legacy.

As the battle raged into the late morning, the sun ascended to its zenith, casting stark shadows across the battlefield strewn with the fallen. The sisters, surrounded by the chaos of combat, continued to fight with a ferocity that belied their exhaustion.

Sumiko, her arm bandaged hastily to stem the flow from her wound, commanded the front lines with an intensity that rallied her fellow villagers. Each motion of her naginata was precise, a deadly grace under pressure that inspired those around her. She anticipated enemy moves with an almost uncanny foresight, her tactics adapting swiftly to the changing tide of battle.

At one point, she found herself surrounded by a group of imperial soldiers. With a calm that seemed out of place in the chaos, she spun, her naginata extending in a wide arc. The blade met armor and flesh, her movements a dance of death. As she turned, her eyes met those of a young soldier, barely older than she. For a moment, the world seemed to slow, the noise dimmed, and Sumiko saw the fear in the young man's eyes—a mirror of her own. With a reluctant resolve, she pushed forward, her blade finding its mark, and the soldier fell. This moment of hesitation was brief but poignant, a stark reminder of the humanity behind each face.

Misako moved through the battlefield like a storm unleashed. Each swing of her katana cleared space around her, her shouts blending with the clash of steel. She was an embodiment of her father's teachings on the Bushido spirit, her ferocity born of a deep-seated belief in her cause. Yet, as the battle wore on, the toll on her body became evident. Her movements, though still lethal, were slower, more deliberate. She grunted as a sword nicked her side, the pain a sharp contrast to the adrenaline that fueled her.

In a particularly brutal encounter, Misako faced off against an imperial officer. Their blades clashed with a sound like thunder, sparks flying. The officer was skilled, but Misako's determination was unyielding. They exchanged blows, each parry and thrust a test of wills. Finally, with a powerful cry, Misako found an opening, her blade driving deep into her adversary's chest. As he collapsed, she paused, her breath heaving, her eyes scanning the battlefield for her sisters, always aware of their presence.

Aiko, though less physically imposing, used her cunning to great effect. She laid traps across the battlefield, her understanding of terrain and enemy patterns allowing her to predict their movements. With a group of younger villagers, she orchestrated a series of hit-and-run tactics that harassed the enemy, sowing confusion and fear.

During a critical moment, Aiko spotted a detachment of armed men attempting to flank the village defenses. Without hesitation, she raised a hand—two fingers up, then a sweep—signaling her group to reposition. They moved in unison, using trees, elevation, and narrow paths to turn the terrain into a weapon.

From a low ridge, Aiko's arrows flew in quick succession—clean, silent, and devastating. Her precision left no time for second chances. There was no panic in her movements, only calculation. Every shift in wind, every rustle of movement, was measured.

As the clash drew closer, she came upon a wounded villager, his leg torn open and trembling in the dirt. She knelt beside him, pulled a broken spear haft from the mud, and fastened a quick splint with cloth torn from her sleeve. Her eyes locked with his. She pressed her hand firmly to his shoulder—not just to steady him, but to speak the words she couldn't voice.

Stay alive. We're still here. You're not alone.

As noon passed, the intensity of the battle did not wane. The ground was slick with blood, the air filled with the cries of the wounded. The sisters, each in their own way, continued to fight, their bodies weary, their spirits battered but unbroken.

The battle was far from over, the outcome uncertain. The Hayashi sisters, linked by blood and battle, fought on, their resolve as sharp as the blades they wielded. They were warriors, yes, but also daughters of a village that relied on their strength and wisdom. Each strike, each maneuver, was a testament to their father's teachings and the fierce love they bore for their home.

The relentless battle for the village wore on as the sun began its descent, casting an eerie light that seemed to paint the battlefield in hues of orange and red, resembling a canvas of war. The Hayashi sisters remained steadfast amidst the chaos, each moment testing their limits and deepening their resolve. As the day wore on, the toll of the battle became evident on every face and in every weary movement. Despite their exhaustion, the sisters continued to fight, driven by a powerful sense of duty and protection for their home. The battlefield was a testament to their courage, strewn with the consequences of war yet underscored by moments of profound bravery and sacrifice.

5: The Abduction

As the dust began to settle on the battlefield, the echoes of chaos still hung in the air like smoke. The attackers—men in mismatched gear, some clad in imperial uniforms, others little more than armed ronin—began a disorganized retreat, scrambling to cover their withdrawal. Scattered across the field, the Hayashi sisters pushed forward, ensuring no further threat lingered in the shadows.

The village, though scarred, stood resilient. Sumiko and Misako, standing on higher ground, watched as the last of the enemy soldiers fled. Relief washed over them briefly, the tension easing from their shoulders as they believed the immediate danger had passed. The villagers started emerging from their hiding spots, the air filled with a cautious jubilation.

Aiko, ever vigilant, moved along the fractured line of defense, her focus on aiding the wounded. Her medical skills were improvised but precise—tourniquets, splints, pressure where it mattered. As she knelt beside a fallen farmer, hands steady against the bleeding, the sudden clash of steel broke the air like a whip. From the treeline, a small group of armed men surged forward—some in partial imperial uniforms, others masked or cloaked, their formation ragged but lethal. It was no organized charge—just a final, desperate strike meant to spill blood during retreat.

Before Aiko could react fully, the trap closed. The attackers moved fast—too fast for a disorganized retreat. Their coordination betrayed intent. She twisted to escape, dropping one with a well-placed arrow to the chest, another with a heel to the knee that sent him crashing into the dirt. But they'd come prepared. One seized her arm, another struck from behind. She fought like a cornered fox—precise, brutal, silent—but the numbers were too many. The bow was ripped from her grip. Her legs kicked out once more, then darkness.

From across the field, Sumiko and Misako saw the abduction unfold. Horror etched on their faces as they sprinted towards their sister, cutting down any enemy that stood in their path. Sumiko's naginata moved with lethal precision, clearing a path through the chaos, while Misako's katana swung in wide, deadly arcs.

Despite their efforts, the distance was too great, and the kidnappers were many. By the time they reached the spot where Aiko had been taken, only the disturbed earth and signs of struggle remained. Misako slammed her fist into the ground, her rage palpable, while Sumiko scanned the horizon, her mind racing for a strategy.

Realizing the gravity of the situation, the sisters quickly rallied a group of villagers, forming a search party. The tracks were fresh, leading into the dense forest that bordered the village. Without a moment's hesitation, Sumiko led the charge, her eyes sharp, her jaw set. Misako, usually the more impulsive one, took a moment to gather her composure, her role as the protector now more crucial than ever.

The forest loomed large as they entered, the shadows deepening as the sun dipped below the horizon. Every snapped twig or rustled leaf heightened their senses. The pursuit was not just a rescue mission but a race against time, as every moment increased the danger Aiko faced.

As they pushed deeper into the forest, the trail became more difficult to follow. The kidnappers knew their path well, utilizing tricks to mask their passage. Misako's frustration grew, her earlier battle fury now channeled into determination. Sumiko remained focused, using every skill her father had taught her to track the faintest signs of passage.

The forest's oppressive silence was a stark contrast to the day's earlier turmoil, the tension mounting with each step. The sisters, their resolve as strong as their blades, moved with a single purpose—rescue Aiko at all costs.

The search through the forest grew more frantic as nightfall enveloped the world in darkness. Sumiko, Misako, and their hastily formed search party pushed through the underbrush, their eyes straining in the dim light, hearts pounding with urgency. The forest, usually a place of solace and quiet, now seemed to mock their desperation with its silence.

Despite their best efforts, the trail grew cold. The kidnappers had covered their tracks expertly, leaving no discernible signs after a certain point.
Sumiko, always the strategist, paused to assess their situation. She knew continuing blindly could lead to further danger or

dilute their efforts. The frustration among the search party was palpable, the fear for Aiko's safety growing with every passing minute.

Misako, unable to hide her distress, lashed out, her voice a harsh whisper in the quiet of the forest. "We can't just give up! She's out there, alone and scared!" Her eyes, usually fierce and determined, now shimmered with tears of rage and helplessness. Sumiko placed a steady hand on her sister's shoulder, her own expression grave. "We will find her, Misako. But we need to think clearly. Blindly searching will only put us all at risk."

With heavy hearts, the party turned back towards the village, the weight of their unspoken fears pressing down on them. As they retraced their steps, the silence of the night was punctuated by the sounds of their subdued footfalls and the distant calls of nocturnal creatures.

Back in the village, the reality of Aiko's abduction settled in like a cold fog. The villagers, already exhausted from the day's battle, gathered around, their faces etched with concern and sorrow. Sumiko addressed the weary crowd, her voice steady despite the turmoil within. "We will regroup and plan. We are not defeated, and we will not rest until Aiko is back with us."

In the dim light of the village meeting hall, lit only by a few flickering lanterns, the sisters convened with the village elders. Maps were spread out, and reports from scouts were shared, each piece of information analyzed for any clue that could lead them to Aiko.

Sumiko led the discussion, her mind working through scenarios, while Misako paced restlessly. The debate was intense, with several plans proposed and discarded.

As the meeting dispersed, the sisters stood together, looking out over the village. The night was quiet, but the peace was deceptive. Inside, a storm of worry and determination raged. Sumiko turned her look to Misako, we will find her. No matter what it takes.

Misako nodded, her resolve hardening. "Yes, we will. They don't know the strength of the Hayashi sisters."

•••

6: Captive Shadows

In a stark contrast to the village's vigil, Aiko found herself plunged into a nightmarish reality. The small fortress to which she was taken loomed like a specter in the diminishing light, its stone walls cold and unyielding. Dragged through its grim corridors, her captors showed no mercy, their grip on her arms tight and punishing.

Once inside the fortress, Aiko was thrown into a small, dank cell, the air thick with the stench of mold and despair. The sound of the heavy door slamming shut echoed ominously, a grim punctuation to her dire situation. Her heart pounded fiercely, not just from fear but from a rising, indignant anger.

Her captors were cruel, their faces twisted with malice. They chained her to the wall, the cold metal biting into her wrists, a stark reminder of her helplessness. The leader of the group, a man with a scar running down his face, leaned close, his breath foul. "You will tell us everything you know about your village's defenses," he sneered, his words a venomous hiss.

When Aiko remained defiant, refusing to speak, the first blow came—a harsh slap that sent her head reeling. Yet, despite the pain, she set her jaw, her resolve hardening. Each subsequent hit was meant to break her, but with each strike, her silent resolve grew stronger.

The torture escalated quickly. They used methods designed to inflict maximum pain without leaving fatal wounds. Cold water was thrown over her repeatedly, chilling her to the bone and leaving her shivering uncontrollably on the stone floor. Her captors watched with cruel amusement, enjoying the power they wielded.

One of them produced a small knife, the blade glinting ominously in the dim light. They didn't cut her—not yet. Instead, they held the blade close, letting her feel its cold edge against her skin, threatening deeper, more grievous harm. They asked again about the village, about her sisters, trying to pry information that could lead to another attack.

Aiko clenched her teeth, the pain and fear mingling with a fierce determination. She thought of her sisters, of her father, of the villagers who depended on them. This thought steeled her against the fear that clawed at her mind.

Days turned into a week, each passing hour a cycle of hope and despair. The small cell became her world, defined by the relentless cycle of interrogation and abuse. Despite her captors' efforts to break her spirit, Aiko's will remained unbroken. Her body was bruised, her muscles ached, and her skin was marred by the cruel ministrations of her captors, but her spirit, that core of iron resolve, remained intact.

Each night, as she lay on the hard, cold floor, Aiko would close her eyes and imagine the faces of her sisters, their voices a comforting echo in her mind. She imagined Sumiko's steady gaze, Misako's fiery spirit, and it gave her strength. In her darkest moments, these visions were a balm, a reminder of who she was and why she must endure.

The torture continued, each session more brutal than the last. Her captors grew increasingly frustrated with her resilience, their methods becoming more desperate and barbaric. Yet, through it all, Aiko held onto a single, unwavering truth—her sisters would come for her. They would not rest until they found her. This belief, this unshakeable faith in her family, fortified her against the waves of pain and despair.

As another dawn approached, bringing light to the darkness of her cell, Aiko braced herself for another day. The pain was a constant companion, but so was her resolve. She would survive this, she had to—for her sisters, for her village, for herself.

The grim days stretched into a seemingly endless ordeal for Aiko, each moment in captivity a stark reminder of her vulnerability yet also a testament to her unyielding spirit. Despite the overwhelming odds, she clung to her inner strength, drawing upon every memory of her family and every lesson her father had taught them about resilience.

In the depths of the fortress, the damp, stone walls of her cell seemed to close in on her, the chill seeping deep into her bones. Her captors' methods grew increasingly cruel, their frustration with her steadfast silence fueling their brutality. One torturer, a tall, gaunt man with cold eyes, seemed particularly intent on breaking her spirit.

This day, he brought with him tools that spoke of unspeakable pain—a set of iron tongs heated in a fire until they glowed ominously. Aiko's heart raced as he approached, the heat from the tongs scorching the air around her. With a malicious grin, he hovered the glowing metal near her skin, the radiant heat causing her to flinch in anticipation of the pain. Yet, before the tongs could touch her, he withdrew them, the threat alone a psychological torment that left her shaking.

Despite the dire circumstances, Aiko's resolve did not waver. She knew that showing fear or pain would only encourage her captors. Instead, she focused her mind, using meditation techniques she had learned in the dojo to distance herself from the immediate threat. She imagined herself beside her sisters, training in the peaceful surroundings of their village, a stark contrast to the dark reality she faced.

Later, the torturers returned, this time forcing her to endure stretches of isolation in complete darkness, the silence of the cell broken only by the occasional drip of water. Time lost meaning, each second stretching into eternity. The isolation was designed to wear her down, to make her crave even the slightest human contact—even if it was from her captors.

But Aiko turned even this torment to her advantage. She retreated into her mind, recalling the stories her father had told them of legendary warriors who faced great adversities with unwavering courage. She constructed mental scenarios, engaging in silent dialogues with her sisters, debating strategies, and recalling happier times. These mental exercises not only kept her spirit intact but also sharpened her mind, preparing her for any possibility.

One night, as the cell door creaked open for the umpteenth time, Aiko steeled herself for another round of questioning. The scar-faced leader entered, his presence as menacing as ever. "This can all end, little bird," he cooed mockingly. "Just tell us what we want to know." His tone was sugary with false sweetness, a stark contrast to the harshness of his usual demeanor.

Aiko met his gaze with a level stare, her voice steady despite her ragged appearance. "I have nothing to say to you," she declared, her voice echoing slightly in the damp cell. It was a simple statement, but it was spoken with a conviction that resonated in the cramped space.

Her captor's face twisted into a snarl, his approach to breaking her obviously failing. He left the cell in a huff, slamming the door behind him, leaving Aiko in the cold darkness once again. But she was not truly alone; her spirit, bolstered by the thoughts of her loved ones and her unshakeable will, kept her company.

As another day broke over the fortress, light creeping into her cell in thin slivers, Aiko prepared herself for whatever trials awaited her. No matter the pain or fear, she would face it head-on, her spirit unbroken, her mind sharp. She was a daughter of the Hayashi, and she would not yield.

•••

Back in the village, under the shadow of the recent battle, the home of the Hayashi sisters felt unusually still. Sumiko and Misako sat across from each other, their faces lit only by the flickering light of a single lantern. The room, usually filled with the echoes of their sisterly banter, now resonated with a tense silence, heavy with worry for Aiko.

Misako looked down, her fingers nervously twisting a piece of cloth, her voice barely a whisper, "What if we can't find her? What if... what if they're hurting her right now?"

Sumiko's response came through her expressive eyes and the quick, determined motions of her hands, her sign language sharp and precise. We must believe she's strong, she signed. Aiko is smart and resourceful. She's surviving this, I know it.

Misako's eyes flicked up to meet her sister's, her expression tormented. "But the thought of her alone, in pain—it's tearing me apart. We should have protected her better."

Sumiko's face softened, her signing gentle. We did everything we could. We fought as hard as we could. Now we need to keep strong, for her.

"But she's the youngest, Sumi. She's always been the one we're supposed to look out for," Misako's voice cracked, her strong facade crumbling as she voiced her deepest fears.

Sumiko reached across the table, her hand squeezing Misako's. Her next message was silent but powerful. Aiko would not want us to fall apart. We owe it to her to stay strong and hopeful.
Misako nodded slowly, wiping away a tear that had escaped down her cheek. "You're right. She's tough—tougher than I give her credit for sometimes.

We've taught her well, and she knows how to endure."

The sisters sat together, drawing comfort from their shared

presence. Memories of Aiko, vibrant and clever, filled the room, momentarily easing the weight of their anxiety.

Misako eventually spoke again, her voice steadier, "Do you remember how she outsmarted us during training last spring? How she managed to pin both of us in under five minutes?"

Sumiko's lips quirked into a small smile, her hands moving with a hint of their usual humor. She's always been the clever one. She's using that now, I'm sure of it.

The night deepened around them, but the sisters found a semblance of peace in their shared memories and the unspoken promise between them. They would find a way to bring Aiko back, not through plans spoken tonight, but through the bond that tied their spirits together. Aiko was part of them, and they would fight the world to bring her home.

...

In the chilling solitude of her cell, Aiko leaned against the cold, damp stone wall, her body aching from the relentless torture. Her mind, however, refused to succumb to the darkness that her captors intended to envelop her in.

Instead, she found solace in thoughts of Sumiko and Misako, the bond they shared as sisters providing a beacon of hope amidst the despair.

Each painful moment was countered by Aiko's vivid memories of her sisters. She remembered Sumiko's silent strength, the way she could communicate so much with just a look or a gesture, her leadership not needing words to inspire confidence. Aiko smiled faintly, recalling how Sumiko could make her feel safe with just a sign, how she had always been the anchor in their dynamic.

Then there was Misako, with her fiery spirit and unyielding courage. Aiko could almost hear her sister's battle cries, echoing in her mind like a war drum, pushing her to not give in. Misako's passionate protectiveness had always been a source of comfort, and now, the memory of it fueled Aiko's determination to withstand her ordeal.

As Aiko sat in the darkness, she closed her eyes and imagined training sessions with her sisters back in their village dojo. She could see Sumiko's focused expression, Misako's enthusiastic movements, and the laughter they shared after a hard day's practice. These memories were vivid, painted in bright colors against the stark gray of her current reality.

She thought about the lessons they had learned together, the stories of legendary warriors who faced great odds with valor and wisdom. These tales, once just stories, now formed the tapestry of her resilience. Aiko drew upon these lessons, using them to fortify her spirit against the hopelessness that tried to creep in.

In her solitude, Aiko held silent dialogues with her sisters. She imagined telling Sumiko about her fears, knowing her elder sister would sign back words of strength and strategy. She pictured Misako's fiery responses, urging her to fight back and keep her chin up. These imagined conversations kept her connected to her sisters, their familiar voices a comforting presence in her mind.

As the night progressed, Aiko's cell remained shrouded in darkness, both literal and metaphorical. Yet, within her, a light persisted—fueled by the love for her sisters and the unbreakable bond they shared. She clung to the belief that Sumiko and Misako were out there, searching for her, planning her rescue. This belief was her armor against the despair, the knowledge that she was not forgotten, that she would not be left behind.

She whispered to herself, a quiet vow in the darkness, "Hold on, Aiko. They are coming for you. Be strong, as they would be for you."

The night slowly ebbed away, each passing moment a step closer to a new day. Aiko, despite her physical exhaustion and pain, remained mentally vigilant, her spirit unbroken. She was a Hayashi, a daughter of warriors, and she would endure. She must.

...

As the village began its slow recovery from the battle's aftermath, an unexpected glimmer of hope reached Sumiko and Misako. A servant working at a nearby fortress had overheard guards talking about a captive girl fitting Aiko's description. He sought out the Hayashi sisters to relay what he had heard. The description matched Aiko too closely to be mere coincidence.

The news ignited a spark of hope in their hearts—the first since Aiko's abduction. But their father, hearing it, didn't share their optimism. His expression remained hard, his tone sharper than before.

"It's a heavily guarded fortress," he said, the weight of

command in every word. "Nearly fifty soldiers... or men dressed like them. Don't mistake a uniform for legitimacy." And I have been ordered to join the forces of the Shogun at Aizu."

He looked at each of his daughters in turn, his pride mingling with a father's worry. "You are onna-musha, trained to protect our home and our people. You must stay and ensure the village's safety. Do not attempt anything reckless."

Misako's eyes filled with tears of frustration. "But father, how can we sit idle while Aiko suffers alone? How can we call ourselves protectors if we do not protect our own?"

Sumiko, constrained by her inability to speak, responded with a series of expressive gestures, her hands cutting through the air with precise, almost poetic movements.

Drawing upon the deepest reserves of her silent voice, she conveyed her dissent:

If words were leaves, I'd scatter them wide, Through winds and whispers, they'd turn the tide.
And should these leaves ignite to flame, They'd light the dark, call out her name.

Her father, moved yet resolute, sighed deeply. "I know your hearts," he said softly, understanding their pain yet bound by duty. "And I trust in your skills. But remember, the honor of the Hayashi name is in your hands. Be wise, be cautious."

Both sisters nodded, their agreement heavy with unspoken resolve. They watched in silence as he prepared for his departure, grappling with the conflict between their duty to their village and their desperate need to save Aiko.

As their father rode out of the village, his figure a fading shadow against the horizon, the sisters shared a silent, somber moment. While they respected his wishes, the thought of leaving Aiko to her fate was unbearable. Yet, bound by the promise they had made to their father, they remained, their hearts torn between duty and the fierce pull of sisterly love.

The decision to stay was made with heavy hearts and a clear understanding of their father's fears. But inside, a fire kindled— a spark of defiance, a whisper of an upcoming storm.

As the echoes of their father's departure faded into the distance, Sumiko and Misako found themselves in the quiet solitude of their family home, each sister wrestling with the command to remain behind. The weight of their father's words, heavy with duty and caution, hung between them like a thick fog.

Misako paced the room, her restlessness palpable. "How can we just stay here while Aiko is out there somewhere, suffering? Isn't it our duty as her sisters, as onna-bugeisha, to go to her aid?" Her voice was thick with emotion, her usual fierceness tinged with desperation.

Sumiko responded, her hands moving in fluid, expressive gestures. Through her sign language, she conveyed her inner turmoil: Duty binds us here, to protect these lands and our people. But the bond of blood, the call of sisterhood—how can we ignore it? Her signs were poignant, capturing the depth of her conflict without a single spoken word.

Misako stopped pacing and looked at her sister, her expression softening. "I know father said we must protect the village, uphold our honor as warriors here. But doesn't honor also call us to protect those we love? How can we honor our family by leaving one of our own in danger?"

Sumiko paused, her fingers weaving through the air with poetic grace, crafting an argument that went beyond words. The Bushido speaks of loyalty and courage. Are we being loyal if we ignore Aiko's plight? Is it courageous to sit here while fear eats at our hearts?

Misako knelt beside her sister, taking her hands in her own. "You're right. The true test of our courage isn't just in battle. It's in making the hard choices, the ones that might lead us into danger because it's where we're needed most."

Their conversation deepened as they discussed the tenets of Bushido, weighing each principle against their desire to act. Loyalty, justice, courage—all seemed to lead back to the same conclusion.

Sumiko's hands moved with a calm certainty. If we stay, we obey one order but betray ourselves and Aiko. Our hearts know the path we must walk, even if it's shrouded in peril.

Misako nodded, her resolve hardening. "We are the daughters of a great samurai, trained not just to fight, but to know why we fight. We fight for family, for honor, and for love. We will go for Aiko, not because it is easy, but because it is right."

The sisters sat together in a powerful silence, the decision made. No plans were discussed yet, no strategies laid out. For now, it was enough to have chosen their path—one led not by orders, but by the unbreakable bonds of family and the deep-seated values that had been instilled in them from a young age.

Their conversation, rich in emotion and steeped in the traditions of their upbringing, reaffirmed their commitment to each other and to their sister. They would stand together, come what may.

•••

As the days turned to weeks, Aiko's captivity stretched on, each moment dragging into the next with excruciating slowness. Confined within the cold, damp walls of her cell in the fortress, her body bore the brutal testament of her ordeal. Wounds, both fresh and partially healed, marred her skin, each one a stark reminder of the relentless torture she endured.

With no way of knowing the world beyond her dark confines, Aiko's mind teetered on the brink of despair. The isolation was suffocating, and in the absence of any news, her imagination conjured the worst scenarios. She feared not only for her own life but for the safety of her sisters. Had they tried to come for her and met with disaster? The thought was unbearable.

In the dead of night, when the fortress lay silent except for the occasional shift of a guard or the distant clink of chains, Aiko allowed herself to feel the full weight of her loneliness. Her body ached from the rough stone floor, her muscles cramped and stiff. Each breath was a sharp pain, and the chill in the air made her shiver uncontrollably.

Despite the physical torment, it was the uncertainty about her sisters that gnawed at her most viciously. Could Sumiko and Misako believe I am dead? she wondered. Have they given up on me, thinking it too dangerous, or worse, have they themselves fallen in an attempt to save me? The possibility of her sisters risking their lives for her was both a comfort and a curse, a source of pride but also of profound terror.

Aiko tried to cling to her training, to the lessons of resilience and inner strength that her father and her sisters had instilled in her. But as the days passed, her spirit, though not broken, frayed at the edges. She found herself talking to her sisters in her mind, imagining conversations, replaying memories of better times. These mental dialogues were her only solace, a fragile thread connecting her to the life she feared she might never return to.

Her physical weakness was mirrored by a growing sense of helplessness. Every sound of the key turning in the lock brought a fresh wave of dread. Each interrogation session was a trial, her captors' faces becoming increasingly blurred in her vision as pain clouded her senses. They demanded information she did not have, accused her of lies she had not told, and with each refusal to cooperate, the punishments grew harsher.

Yet, even in her darkest moments, Aiko's thoughts returned to her sisters. They would not give up, she told herself. Neither will I. This resolve was her armor against despair, the mantra she repeated with every painful breath. Even if she felt forgotten by the world, she would not let herself be erased.

She would survive, if not for herself, then for the hope that one day, somehow, her sisters might find her.

As another dawn crept into her cell, the weak light barely

illuminating the stark confines, Aiko braced herself for another day. Her body was battered, her spirit beleaguered, but not defeated. She would endure, hold on to the sliver of hope that Sumiko and Misako were still out there, fighting for her as she was fighting to survive in the darkness.

...

7: Night of the Vegenful Shadow

Under the veil of a torrential downpour, two dark figures moved with silent precision through the shadows of the night. Cloaked entirely in black, they were barely discernible against the backdrop of the dense forest that bordered the fortress. Raindrops fell heavily, drumming against the leaves and the muddy earth, masking the sound of their cautious movements.

The fortress loomed ahead, its imposing stone walls rising stark against the dark sky, the occasional torchlight flickering along the ramparts where guards patrolled. The figures paused, melding into the darkness beneath a large oak, their eyes fixed on the patterns of the guards' movements. They watched intently, noting the timing of the patrols and the changing of the guard, every detail meticulously observed.

These were no ordinary intruders; they were predators of the night—deadly, determined. The rain soaked through their cloaks, but they remained unmoved, their focus unyielding.

Each movement was deliberate, calculated to bring them closer to their prey without alerting the fortress's defenders.

As they approached the fortress's outer wall, one figure pointed upwards towards a lone guard atop the rampart, his attention fixed on the opposite side, oblivious to the danger lurking just below. The figures crouched low, communicating through subtle hand signals before moving forward with renewed purpose.

For this night, Sumiko and Misako had shed their identities as onna-musha, the honorable female warriors of their village, and donned the guise of shinobis. This transformation was not just physical but a profound shift in their approach to combat and duty. Where the onna-musha upheld the Bushido code with openness and honor, shinobis operated in the shadows, valuing stealth and secrecy to achieve their objectives.

This decision to embrace the way of the shinobi was driven by desperation and a deep, unyielding love for their sister. They knew that infiltrating a heavily guarded fortress required more than just bravery and skill; it demanded the cunning and shadowy tactics of the shinobi. For Sumiko and Misako, this night's mission transcended the traditional boundaries of the Bushido code they lived by. It was a necessary departure from their principles, dictated by the dire circumstances and their single-minded resolve to rescue Aiko.

As they prepared to scale the fortress wall, the rain continued to pour, washing over them like a cloak of darkness, concealing their presence. They were shadows in the storm, two sisters against a fortress of foes, their hearts beating not just for survival but for the family they were determined to reunite.

Under the cloak of a relentless downpour and the cover of deep darkness, Sumiko and Misako began their perilous ascent of the fortress wall. The rain had turned the ancient stones slick, but their grip was firm, their movements deliberate and silent. Each sister used the small crevices and protrusions in the stonework as holds, pulling themselves up with a grace and efficiency honed by years of training.

Reaching the top of the wall was only the first challenge. As Sumiko's head crested the parapet, her eyes quickly scanned for the lone guard whose attention had previously been fixed away from their approach. He stood just a few paces away, his body obscured by the heavy rain and the darkness.

Sumiko signaled to Misako, marking their first target.

Without a sound, Sumiko pulled herself over the wall, her movements fluid and ghost-like. As she approached the unsuspecting guard from behind, her hand drew a small, sharp dagger from her belt. With a swift, precise movement, she covered the guard's mouth with one hand and drew the blade across his throat with the other. The guard's body tensed and then slumped as she gently lowered him to the ground, ensuring the silence of their infiltration remained unbroken.

Misako, following closely, had now also scaled the wall and was assessing their next move. The fortress's ramparts were patrolled intermittently by four more guards, each spaced out along the walkway. The sisters divided their tasks with a nod, each taking responsibility for two guards.

Misako moved towards the next guard, her steps nearly soundless even in the puddles that dotted the stone walkway. As she neared her target, she withdrew a thin garrote wire from her sleeve. Timing her approach with a gust of wind that howled over the ramparts, she slipped the wire over the guard's head and tightened it swiftly. The struggle was brief; Misako's technique left no room for noise or prolonged conflict.

Meanwhile, Sumiko had circled around a small turret to approach another guard. Utilizing the shadows cast by the battlements, she closed the distance between them with predatory precision. As she reached him, her hand shot out, striking pressure points on the guard's neck with debilitating accuracy. He collapsed instantly, silently, his body barely making a sound as it hit the wet stone.

The final guard was the most challenging, positioned as he was with a panoramic view of the approach. Both sisters converged to handle this last obstacle together. Misako distracted him with a subtle noise—a thrown pebble tapping against the far wall. As the guard turned to investigate the sound, Sumiko approached from behind, her dagger ready. The kill was clean and efficient, a testament to their skill and their grim determination.

With the wall guards silently neutralized, Sumiko and Misako paused to regroup, their breathing steady despite the adrenaline that coursed through their veins. They had turned the fortress wall into a silent tableau of their lethal efficiency, each guard dispatched without alert or alarm.

The sisters shared a brief look, a mutual understanding of the gravity of their actions and the necessity of their mission. They were deep in enemy territory now, far from the safety of their village and the guiding principles of their father's teachings. Yet, the necessity of their actions, driven by the desperate need to save Aiko, justified the darkness of their methods this night.

As they prepared to descend into the heart of the fortress, the rain continued to pour down, washing away any trace of their grim work atop the wall.

Under the cloak of the relentless downpour, Sumiko and Misako swiftly assessed the layout of the fortress from their vantage point atop the wall. The rain masked their movements, allowing them to move invisibly through the shadows. They knew their next target had to be strategic: the fortress's commander, stationed in his quarters on the second floor, engaged in discussion with two of his lieutenants. Eliminating the leadership could sow enough confusion to aid their mission.

They descended silently from the wall, sticking close to the wet stone surfaces, blending into the darkness. Their path was meticulously chosen to avoid the main areas of activity—soldiers gathered around a campfire, their laughter and chatter echoing faintly through the rain, a group of guards chatting near the stables, and the distant barks of guard dogs tied near the main gate.

The sisters moved with lethal precision, taking out a lone guard who patrolled the back corridors. Sumiko, leading the way, signaled Misako to follow as they approached the barracks where some soldiers were sleeping. Using a series of hand signals, they coordinated their movements, ensuring they remained undetected.

Their next encounter was near the kitchens, where two guards stood talking under the cover of an awning, trying to stay dry. Misako approached from behind, her movements a whisper against the storm's howl. Her hands were swift and sure, a garrote wire slipping silently around the first guard's neck, pulling tight. Sumiko dealt with the second guard, her dagger finding the soft space beneath his jaw, silencing him before a sound could escape his lips.

With the perimeter guards neutralized, they made their way towards the main building, their clothes heavy with rain, their hearts heavier with the gravity of their task. The commander's room was on the second floor, overlooking the central courtyard. They entered the building through a service door, used primarily by the servants during the day. The narrow staircase was dimly lit by flickering oil lamps, casting long shadows on the walls.

As they ascended, the muffled sounds of the commander's voice became clearer. He was discussing troop movements, his voice authoritative and unaware of the danger creeping ever closer. Sumiko and Misako paused at the top of the stairs, listening for a moment to gauge the positions of the men inside.

Choosing their moment, they burst through the door. Misako threw a small, homemade flash device into the center of the room, a simple concoction of blinding powder and a small spark. As the room erupted in a flash of light and a loud bang, the sisters charged. The disoriented men barely had time to react. Sumiko tackled the lieutenant closest to the door, her hand clamped over his mouth as she drove her dagger deep into his side, angling it to ensure a swift demise. Misako engaged the commander, her katana clashing against his in a brief, fierce exchange. The sound of steel on steel rang out, a deadly dance that ended with Misako's blade at the commander's throat. The second lieutenant, scrambling to draw his weapon, was met by Sumiko's silent but deadly approach, her dagger finding his heart.

With the room secured and the commander and his lieutenants down, Sumiko and Misako quickly rifled through the documents on the desk, searching for any information that might indicate where Aiko was being held. Their movements were efficient, every second counting. Amidst various military dispatches and orders, they found a document with Aiko's name—a report stating that the interrogation and torture had been fruitless and that an execution order had been issued, though no date was specified.

The room seemed to spin as the weight of the words struck them. Misako's hands trembled as she held the paper, her voice barely a whisper, "Sumiko, is she... could she already be...?"

Sumiko, unable to speak, felt a sharp pain clutch at her heart. Her hands shook as she signed, her movements jerky with shock and despair. We don't know. There's no date. She could still be alive.

Misako's eyes, filled with a tormenting mix of hope and dread, met her sister's. "But what if we're too late? What if we—"

We can't think like that, Sumiko signed back fiercely. We have to believe she's alive. We have to keep going.

"But if they've hurt her, if they've... if she's gone, Sumiko, I can't—I won't just stand by," Misako's voice cracked, the grief and rage building like a storm inside her.

Sumiko reached out, grabbing her sister's hand, her own emotions a turbulent whirl. She signed with a resolve that left no room for doubt. Then we avenge her. We make them pay. This isn't just a rescue mission anymore.

Misako nodded, her jaw set in a hard line as tears streaked down her cheeks, mingling with the rain. "No, it's not. They took our sister from us. If Aiko is... if we're too late, then we'll make sure every single one of them regrets the day they touched her."

The mood in the room shifted palpably, the air charged with a raw, seething anger. The mission had changed, evolved not just out of necessity but out of a deep, unyielding fury. They were no longer just sisters trying to save their family; they were avenging angels, ready to unleash their wrath.

Sumiko signed, her movements sharp and decisive. We finish this tonight. For Aiko. Misako picked up her katana, her grip tightening around the hilt. "For Aiko," she echoed, her voice a mix of sorrow and determination. "They will all pay."

The sisters took one last look at the documents, memorizing everything they needed before leaving the room. Their steps were purposeful, their hearts heavy but fueled by a newfound determination. As they moved through the darkened corridors of the fortress, every shadow and every sound was a call to arms—a reminder of why they were there and what they had to do.

The fortress, once just a structure of stone and wood, had become the arena of their vengeance. And as they moved deeper into its heart, they carried with them not just the hope of finding Aiko alive but the certainty that no matter the outcome, no enemy would walk away unscathed.

•••

As Sumiko and Misako stepped silently into the room where a dozen soldiers lay sleeping, their minds were not clouded by hesitation, only fueled by a singular, seething intent: revenge. The rain outside muffled any sound as they approached, shadows amongst shadows, their figures barely discernible in the dimly lit quarters.

Misako was the first to strike, her movements a blend of grace and lethal precision. She approached the nearest sleeping soldier, her katana gleaming faintly in the low light. With a swift, fluid motion, she drew the blade across his throat, the cut so clean and sharp that he barely stirred before life left him. The quiet shh of the blade slicing through air and flesh was soon echoed around the room as she moved from one soldier to the next, her expression set in a grim line, her eyes cold and unyielding.

Sumiko, meanwhile, used her daggers with devastating efficiency. She stood over a soldier, pausing just a moment to ensure her strike would be fatal.

Then, with a quick thrust, she plunged her dagger deep into the soldier's chest, right through the heart. As he gasped his last breath, she was already moving to her next target, her actions methodical, each strike a silent testament to her fury.

Together, the sisters moved through the room like avenging

spirits, their motions synchronized and deadly. Sumiko's technique was quieter, more about precision and minimal movement, while Misako's style was sweeping and fluid, her katana slicing through the air with a dancer's grace.

One soldier, roused by a dying comrade's final breath, barely had time to register the horror before him. He reached for his weapon, a look of dawning terror on his face. Misako met his gaze, her eyes a reflection of the storm raging outside and within. She did not hesitate; her katana swung down in a powerful arc, severing his hand before cutting across his neck, silencing his scream before it could begin.

The room quickly became a tableau of death, the floor stained with spreading pools of blood. Not a single soldier was spared, each man meeting a swift, brutal end. This was not the honorable combat of warriors meeting on a battlefield; this was the dark deed of revenge, born from pain and loss, executed with chilling efficiency.

As the last soldier's body hit the ground, Sumiko and Misako stood amidst the carnage, their breathing heavy, their bodies splattered with the blood of their enemies. There was no satisfaction in their eyes, only the grim resolution of what was yet to come. They had become instruments of vengeance, and this room was merely the first act.

Leaving the room as silently as they had entered, they continued deeper into the fortress. Each step was driven by a relentless, burning desire to avenge Aiko, to make every enemy pay dearly for her suffering. The night was far from over, and their wrath had only just begun to unfold.

•••

In the suffocating darkness of her cell, damp with the relentless seepage of rainwater, Aiko sat huddled against the cold, unforgiving stone. Her body was a map of bruises and cuts, her clothes tattered and stained with the evidence of her prolonged suffering. Despite her physical frailty, the flame of defiance still flickered within her, dimmed but unextinguished.

The heavy thud of boots echoed down the corridor, a sound that had come to herald further torment. The rusty screech of her cell door swinging open broke the heavy silence. The cell master entered, his presence looming like a dark cloud, accompanied by three soldiers. Their faces were twisted into sneers of anticipation, their eyes gleaming cruelly in the dim torchlight that filtered into her small, dismal confines.

The cell master's voice was oily with malice as he approached Aiko, squatting down to her level. "We have some good news for you," he drawled, his breath foul. "This will be your last night here. Tomorrow, you'll be released—not just from this cell, but from your life too." His grin widened, revealing yellowed teeth. "But tonight, we want some fun with you. You are really a very sweet thing, and I've been waiting for this moment for a while."
His hand reached out, caressing her cheek with mock tenderness, a stark contrast to the harsh grip that followed as he grabbed her chin, forcing her to meet his gaze. "Being nice to us will give you a quick end tomorrow.

Otherwise, we can make your end very, very slow," he threatened, his voice a sinister whisper.

Aiko's heart pounded in her chest, fear mingling with a surge of revulsion, but she held his gaze, her own eyes burning with a quiet intensity. She had endured much, and though her body was weak, her spirit harbored reserves of strength that even she hadn't fully realized.

The soldiers laughed, a harsh, grating sound that echoed off the stone walls. One of them stepped forward, unlocking the chains that bound her to the wall. As the cold metal fell away, her arms dropped limply by her sides, the circulation slow to return. They grabbed her arms, pulling her to her feet. She swayed, her legs weak from prolonged immobility, but she forced herself to stand, to face her tormentors with as much dignity as she could muster.

The cell master watched with a vile satisfaction as Aiko struggled to remain upright. "That's it, little bird, time to fly," he mocked, pushing her slightly, enjoying the sight of her battling to maintain balance.

As they prepared to drag her out of the cell, Aiko's mind raced, desperation clawing at the edges of her resolve. The threat of what was to come hung heavily in the air, a palpable terror that would have broken many. Yet, within Aiko, a spark of defiance still smoldered—fueled by thoughts of her sisters, their love and their courage, which even now, she hoped, was bringing them closer to her rescue.

...

In the shadowy depths of the fortress, Sumiko and Misako regrouped, their breaths coming in quick, determined huffs. Their faces, illuminated only by the intermittent flashes of lightning from the storm outside, were set in grim lines of resolve. They had dispatched nearly twenty soldiers with ruthless efficiency, but the realization hung heavily between them that there could be many more. Misako recalled their father's words—fifty soldiers, perhaps more.

"We may face over a hundred," Misako murmured, wiping her blade clean on the fabric of a fallen enemy. "But we will fight, Sumiko. We will fight them all if we have to, or we die trying." Sumiko nodded, her gestures swift and sharp as she signed in return, her eyes fierce and unflinching, *For Aiko. If this is where our path ends, so be it. We make it count.*

Sumiko and Misako, shrouded in the darkness just beyond the reach of the fortress's torchlight, watched the patrol of soldiers round the corner. Their bodies tensed for the impending confrontation, they exchanged a glance, a silent nod signaling their readiness. As the soldiers laughed obliviously, the sisters prepared to strike, transforming from silent shadows into instruments of vengeance.

Misako led the assault, her katana slicing through the humid night air with a deadly hiss. The blade met the neck of the lead soldier, cutting off his laughter in a gurgling choke as he stumbled forward, a look of shocked disbelief etched on his face as he crumpled to the muddy ground. With the grace of a seasoned dancer, Misako pivoted, her weapon arcing through the air to meet the next soldier, her movements so swift and precise they offered no chance for defense or parry.

Sumiko, wielding her daggers with silent precision, approached from behind the patrol. Her target, unaware, barely sensed the faint pressure against his back before her blade punctured his heart. As he dropped silently, she spun fluidly to face another assailant, her dagger tracing a deadly arc across his throat, spraying a fine mist of blood into the rain-soaked air.

But the confrontation was far from over. As the initial group of soldiers lay defeated, three more appeared from the shadows, alerted by the faint noise of the skirmish. These new adversaries were on high alert, their bows drawn, arrows notched as they advanced toward the sounds of their fallen comrades.

The sudden appearance of reinforcements put the sisters at a momentary disadvantage. An arrow whizzed through the air, slicing the space where Sumiko had just been a second before. She rolled to the side, narrowly avoiding another arrow, her heart pounding as the real threat of the situation settled in. Misako, spotting the archers, shouted a warning and charged with her katana raised, closing the distance to prevent them from using their ranged advantage.

The battle became a desperate dance of steel and survival. Misako deflected an arrow with her sword, the metallic clang stark against the softer sounds of the rain. She reached the first archer, her blade sweeping in a wide arc. The soldier tried to parry with his short sword, but Misako's anger fueled her strength, overpowering him quickly, her katana slashing deeply across his torso.

Sumiko engaged the next two soldiers, her daggers a blur of movement. She ducked under an awkwardly aimed sword thrust, stepping in close to deliver a crippling blow to her attacker's knee. As he fell, wailing in pain, she used her momentum to throw him into the other archer, disrupting his aim. With a swift, clean movement, she silenced them both, her daggers finding their lethal marks.

As the last of the new threats fell, the sisters regrouped, breathing heavily, their clothes stained with the blood of their enemies. The fortress, alive with the sounds of their combat, now felt even more like a colossal trap. Yet, the sisters' resolve did not waver; if anything, the close call had only hardened their determination.

"We must be cautious, Misako," Sumiko signed urgently, her hands swift and expressive even in the dim light. "They know we are here now. We must move quickly, but stealthily."

Misako nodded, wiping the rain and sweat from her brow. "Every corridor, every shadow could hold our death, but we push forward. For Aiko."

With grim faces set against the dark, stormy backdrop of the night, Sumiko and Misako continued their harrowing advance through the fortress. The thought that Aiko could already be dead spurred them on, turning their mission from rescue to retribution. Each step was laden with danger, but driven by a ferocious need for vengeance, the sisters moved deeper into the heart of enemy territory, prepared to face whatever horrors lay ahead.

•••

The fortress erupted into chaos as the alarm spread like wildfire through its stone corridors and open courtyards. A soldier, stumbling upon the grim tableau of the dispatched patrol, had sounded the alarm, his shouts piercing the night, rallying the fortress's remaining defenders. In moments, the entire stronghold was awake and on high alert.

Sumiko and Misako, once the hunters moving through the shadows, now found themselves the prey. The roles had reversed with startling speed, and the fortress transformed from a navigable danger to a deadly labyrinth. The sisters, though still lethal and determined, were forced to adapt quickly to their new status as the hunted.

As they darted across a dimly lit courtyard, seeking the dubious shelter of a small outbuilding, the air suddenly thrummed with the sound of a loosed arrow. Misako, caught off guard, felt a sharp sting as the arrow buried itself in her leg. She stumbled, her cry of pain muffled by her determination not to alert more soldiers to their precise location.

"Keep moving!" Misako hissed as Sumiko moved to support her, draping her sister's arm over her shoulder. Every step was a challenge now, Misako's injury slowing them significantly.

They managed to duck into the shadow of an old armory, catching their breath as they assessed the situation. The fortress, alive with the sounds of soldiers calling to one another and the clatter of armor, seemed to close in around them. Sumiko's eyes met Misako's, a silent conversation passing between them in the gloom. We are still predators, Sumiko signed, her movements tight with controlled urgency, but now we must think like prey as well.

Using the armory as a temporary haven, they quickly fashioned a makeshift bandage for Misako's wound. Sumiko tore a strip from her own clothing, binding the wound tightly to stem the flow of blood. Misako gritted her teeth against the pain, her determination not to become a liability burning bright in her eyes.

"We need to move," Misako said through clenched teeth, testing her weight on her injured leg. "If they corner us here, it's over." They exited the armory, moving much more slowly now. Sumiko took the lead, her senses heightened to every shadow and every sound. As they rounded a corner, a shout split the air. "There! The intruders!"

A group of soldiers charged toward them, their weapons drawn and faces set in grim determination. Sumiko and Misako, backs against the wall, faced their attackers. Despite Misako's injury, their stance was resolute, their weapons ready.

The confrontation was fierce and desperate. Sumiko parried and dodged, her dagger finding gaps in armor and flesh. Misako, despite her pain, fought with a ferocious energy, her katana slashing through the air, cutting down anyone who came too close.

But the odds were shifting rapidly against them. More soldiers poured into the area, encircling the sisters. The reality of their situation was stark; they were trapped, wounded, and outnumbered. Yet, their faces showed no sign of surrender, only the steely resolve of warriors prepared to fight to their last breath.

The atmosphere was electric with danger, every moment stretched taut with the imminent threat of death. Sumiko and Misako stood shoulder to shoulder, their breaths mingling in the chill air, their hearts beating not just with fear but with a profound, unyielding courage. The fortress, once just a mission, was now a battlefield, and they were its defiant last stand.

•••

In the dank confines of her cell, Aiko stood, her resolve as steely as the cold, wet walls that imprisoned her. Two soldiers gripped her arms firmly, holding her in place as the cellmaster leered close, his breath foul and his intentions fouler. "So, where should we start?" he murmured, his hand reaching out to caress her face. "Maybe with a little kiss from the little bird?" His smirk was repulsive, his proximity overwhelming.

Disgust churned in Aiko's stomach, her skin crawling under his touch. As he leaned in closer, his lips puckering in a grotesque imitation of affection, Aiko saw her opportunity. With a surge of adrenaline-fueled strength, she snapped her head forward, sinking her teeth into the soft flesh of the cellmaster's cheek. She clamped down hard, tasting blood, feeling the man's flesh tear under the pressure of her bite.

The cellmaster howled in agony, his hands flying to his face as he stumbled backwards. He swung wildly with his backhand, striking Aiko across the face. The force of the blow sent her reeling back onto the cold stone floor, stars bursting in her vision from the impact.

At that moment, the distant sounds of the fortress alarm pierced the air, the clamor echoing through the corridors and reaching the depths of the dungeon. Surprised and momentarily distracted, the cellmaster looked up towards the door, barking orders to his remaining two men. "Check what's going on!" he screamed, clutching his bleeding cheek.

As the two soldiers hurried out, Aiko found herself on the floor, facing the cellmaster and one other guard who hesitated, unsure whether to follow his comrades or stay. Seizing the moment, Aiko sprang into action. No longer shackled, her body surged with a mix of pain and adrenaline. She rolled to the side, avoiding a clumsy attempt by the guard to grab her, and snatched up a small, sharp stone from the floor.

With a fierce cry that was part roar, part scream, Aiko lunged at the guard. The stone, sharp and solid, found its mark in his throat. The guard gurgled, clutching at his bleeding neck, collapsing as he tried to scream for help.

Before the cellmaster could react, still disoriented from his injury and the shock of the alarm, Aiko was on him.

Her movements were fueled by a potent cocktail of fear, anger, and desperate hope. She slammed the stone against the side of the cellmaster's head, stunning him. As he staggered, she pushed him against the wall, her hands searching for any weapon she could find. Her fingers closed around the guard's dropped sword, and with a strength born of desperation, she drove the blade deep into the cellmaster's abdomen.

The cellmaster gasped, his eyes widening in shock and pain. Aiko twisted the blade cruelly, ensuring the wound was fatal. As he slumped to the ground, clutching at the sword impaling him, Aiko stood back, panting, her entire body shaking.

The fortress's alarm continued to ring out, a backdrop to the violent tableau in the cell. Aiko's heart pounded in her chest, each beat a reminder that she was still alive, still fighting, not just for survival, but now, potentially, for rescue.

Her eyes hardened as she pulled the sword from the cellmaster's body, preparing herself for whatever came next. The fortress was in chaos, and though she was wounded and alone, she was free from her chains. Now, it was her turn to hunt.

As Aiko stepped out of her cell, the katana of the fallen guard in her hand felt heavy yet right. The fortress was engulfed in chaos, the alarm's clamor mingling with shouts and the clanging of metal. Wounded, dirty, and bloodied, Aiko's spirit surged with a raw, unbridled force. Her days of captivity had culminated in this moment—freedom was within grasp, and she was determined to seize it.

Navigating the dimly lit corridors, her senses were heightened to every sound and movement. The chaos outside provided the perfect cover, her captors distracted and dispersed, dealing with the threat they couldn't yet understand. Aiko moved with purpose, her footsteps silent despite the urgency that drove her.
As she approached the exit of the prison wing, the two guards who had been sent to investigate the disturbance returned. They rounded the corner, not expecting to meet anyone, especially not a figure from their darkest nightmares—Aiko stood before them, a spectral vision of vengeance, her clothes torn and stained with the blood of their cellmaster, her face smeared with dirt and blood.

The guards halted abruptly, their eyes widening in horror at the sight of the woman they had underestimated, now transformed into an avenger. There was a moment of stunned silence before instinct took over, and they drew their weapons, a feeble attempt to defend themselves.

Aiko's reaction was swift and merciless. With another battle roar, she lunged forward. The first guard barely raised his sword before Aiko's katana met his throat, the blade slicing through flesh and sinew with a brutal efficiency. Blood spurted in an arc, painting the grimy walls red as he collapsed, gurgling and clutching at his severed throat.

The second guard, momentarily frozen by the ferocity of her onslaught, reacted a second too late. Aiko pivoted, the momentum carrying her forward. She parried his desperate swing and countered with a vicious thrust. The katana pierced his chest, driving deep, the impact lifting him off his feet.

Aiko withdrew the blade, and he fell heavily to the floor, his lifeblood pooling around him.

Breathing heavily, Aiko stood between the bodies of her foes, her chest heaving with exertion and adrenaline. The corridor was eerily quiet now, the distant sounds of chaos reminding her that the fortress was still a dangerous labyrinth.

With no time to waste, Aiko resumed her path to the exit, her resolve hardened. Each step was fueled by the years of torment she had endured, each breath a testament to her unyielding spirit. She was no longer just a prisoner, or even a survivor; she was an avenger, carving her path to freedom with the blade that had once been wielded against her.

As she moved through the shadows, her presence was as lethal as the blade she carried—every corner turned, every door breached brought her closer to escape, to survival, to the possibility of reuniting with her sisters.

As Aiko ascended the steps to a higher vantage point within the fortress, she could feel the pulse of the battle resonating through the stone beneath her feet. The chaos of the alarm had drawn every available soldier to the inner courtyard, leaving her path surprisingly clear but fraught with the tension of impending conflict.

Reaching the top of the staircase, she found herself on a section of the wall that overlooked the courtyard. Peering down, her breath caught in her throat at the sight below. There, amidst the chaos, were Sumiko and Misako, backs pressed against each other, surrounded by a swarm of soldiers. They fought with desperate, fierce grace, their katanas flashing in the dim light as they held their ground under a small overhang. It was a temporary respite from the rain of arrows that occasionally sought to find them, arrows that clattered harmlessly on the tiled roof above their heads.

Around the edges of the courtyard, Aiko noticed a line of archers perched on the wall, their bows drawn, aiming into the fray but unable to get a clear shot at her sisters due to their sheltered position. Despite this small mercy, the situation looked dire. Misako's movements were hindered, a noticeable limp hampering her usual agility, likely from the arrow wound Aiko could now see staining her sister's leg with blood. Both sisters bore numerous cuts and bruises, their faces set in grim lines of pain and determination.

From her elevated position, Aiko's heart swelled with a tumultuous mix of pride and fear. Pride, because her sisters had come for her, they had not abandoned her; they had braved the depths of this fortress hell to find her. And fear, because they were now in grave danger, their lives hanging by a thread as thin as the blades they wielded.

Tears blurred her vision, but she blinked them away, her grip tightening on the katana she still held. The sight of her sisters fighting so valiantly, so desperately, ignited a fierce resolve within her. They came all this way for me, she thought, her chest tightening with emotion. They believed I was still alive. They never gave up.

But as she watched them parry and strike, each movement laden with fatigue and pain, the reality of their peril struck her forcefully. What can I do? she asked herself, her mind racing. How can I help them? How can I change the tide of this battle? Aiko knew she couldn't just watch. She needed to act, to do something to tip the scales back in their favor. But from her position, options seemed limited. She scanned the courtyard and the surrounding areas, searching for anything that might be used to her advantage—a dropped weapon, an unattended horse, anything.

The questions whirled in her mind, each one hammering home the urgency of the situation. How can I save them? How can I make sure we all get out of this alive?

As the clash of steel rang out below, mingling with the shouts of men and the cries of the wounded, Aiko steeled herself for whatever came next. She was no longer the captive waiting to be rescued; she was a warrior, a sister, ready to fight for the family she loved so dearly.

With the fortress submerged in chaos and her mind racing for a viable strategy, Aiko realized that improvisation was her only ally. The rain had soaked everything, but the oil lamps that hung along the wall still burned, resilient against the night's dampness. Though weak and recovering from weeks of confinement,

Aiko's determination was undeterred.

With the fortress submerged in chaos and her mind racing for a viable strategy, Aiko realized that improvisation was her only ally. The rain had soaked everything, but the oil lamps that hung along the wall still burned, resilient against the night's dampness. Though weak and recovering from weeks of confinement, Aiko's determination was undeterred. She eyed the burning lamps—a tool provided by the fortress itself that might just help turn the tide in favor of her sisters.

Using her surroundings to her advantage, Aiko carefully removed one of the still-lit lamps from its hook. The flames danced wildly, reflecting a fierce determination in her eyes. Clutching the handle tightly, she moved stealthily along the wall, her steps measured and silent, each movement calculated to avoid drawing attention.

Below, Sumiko and Misako were barely holding their ground, forced into a defensive posture beneath an overhang that shielded them from the archers' arrows but not from the relentless assault by the soldiers. The situation was dire, and Aiko knew she had to act swiftly.

From her elevated position, she targeted the densest cluster of soldiers pressing in on her sisters. With a deep, steadying breath, Aiko swung the lamp with all her might, releasing it to sail through the rain-soaked air. The lamp arced perfectly, crashing into the ground near the soldiers, its oil spilling and the flames catching on their cloaks. The sudden burst of fire caused instant confusion and fear, drawing soldiers away from Sumiko and Misako to deal with the new threat.

Seizing the opportunity, Aiko grabbed another lamp and hurled it toward a group of soldiers trying to flank her sisters from the side. The second lamp broke upon impact, spreading fire across the slick cobblestones, creating a fiery barrier that thwarted the soldiers' movements and funneled them back into the direct line of sight of Sumiko and Misako. The sisters took advantage of the chaos, pressing their attack with renewed vigor, their blades slicing through the disoriented and frightened soldiers.

Encouraged by her success, Aiko continued to rain down fiery havoc upon the enemy troops, using the lamps as makeshift incendiary devices. Each throw was precise, designed to create maximum disruption and give her sisters the upper hand. The courtyard soon became a scene of smoldering chaos, where the fire she set not only illuminated the night but also the desperation of their foes.

•••

As flames engulfed the courtyard, creating a chaotic dance of light and shadow, Sumiko and Misako suddenly realized the source of their unexpected aid. Above, outlined against the glow of the burning oil lamps she wielded like fiery weapons, was Aiko. Her presence, fierce and determined atop the wall, was like a vision amidst the pandemonium.

Misako's heart leapt in her chest, her voice piercing the tumult. "Aiko! She's alive!" The relief and joy in her shout mingled with the intensity of the battle, infusing both sisters with renewed vigor.
But their moment of elation was swiftly tempered by danger. The archers, having recovered from their initial confusion, had

spotted Aiko on the wall. They began to realign their bows, targeting her silhouette against the flickering flames. The threat was immediate and deadly, requiring swift action to protect their sister.

•••

Recognizing the urgency, Sumiko quickly gestured to Misako, her hands slicing through the air with sharp, decisive signs for "attack from distance." Misako nodded, her eyes narrowing as she pulled several shurikens from a pouch at her belt—each small, star-shaped blade gleaming ominously under the firelight. With a deadly calm, she flung the shurikens with precise and swift movements. The blades whirred menacingly through the air, their edges catching the light as they spun towards their targets.

The first shuriken struck an archer square in the throat, slicing through flesh and artery with a gruesome efficiency. The archer's horrified gasp was cut short as blood spurted violently from the wound, his body crumpling silently to the ground. Another shuriken embedded deeply in the eye of a second archer, who screamed in agony, dropping his bow as he clawed desperately at his face, stumbling backwards until he fell over, writhing in the mud.

The last of Misako's thrown blades found its mark in the chest of a third archer, piercing his heart with lethal precision. He dropped instantly, his bow slipping from lifeless fingers as a final breath escaped his lips in a bloody froth. The remaining archers, now acutely aware of the deadly accuracy of these new adversaries, scrambled in disarray, their formation broken as panic overtook their ranks.

Meanwhile, Sumiko charged at another group of soldiers who were attempting to use the chaos as cover to advance. Her katana was a blur of deadly precision, cutting through armor and bone with equal ease. Each strike was a spray of crimson that painted the wet cobblestones red, her movements a dance of death choreographed by necessity and desperation.

The fire Aiko had set was spreading, catching on a nearby stable, causing the horses within to panic. The sound of frightened horses added to the cacophony, and as the stable doors burst open, several startled horses charged out. Their wild escape added a new layer of confusion to the battlefield, providing the sisters a critical distraction. Soldiers scrambled to avoid the rampaging animals, breaking their formation and giving Misako and Sumiko crucial openings to press their attack.

Aiko, from her vantage point, saw the immediate danger posed by the archers refocusing on her. Quickly, she dropped back from the wall's edge, using the smoke and the uneven lighting to obscure her position. She scanned the area, looking for anything else she could use to create further diversions or defend herself. Spotting a rope used to hoist supplies to the wall, she swiftly cut it, sending a stack of crates crashing down onto another group of archers. The impact was devastating, scattering them and effectively taking them out of the fight.

As the flames grew, so did the chaos. The fire not only illuminated the night but also transformed the fortress into a perilous maze of smoke, shadow, and unpredictable danger. Sumiko and Misako, bolstered by Aiko's presence and their reunited purpose, fought back-to-back against the encroaching soldiers. Each sister was an avatar of fury and focus, their movements synchronized in a lethal ballet.

The battle was brutal, the air filled with the sounds of clashing steel, the shouts of men, and the sharp cries of the wounded. Blood flowed freely, mixing with the rainwater to form rivulets of red that washed over the cobblestones. The sisters, united by blood and battle, were a formidable force, their love and loyalty to each other driving them to overcome the overwhelming odds.

In this dire tableau, the sisters were not just fighting for survival but for something far greater—their unbreakable bond, the memory of their suffering, and the chance for vengeance against those who had wronged them so deeply.

In the midst of chaos and flame, Sumiko and Misako carved a path of destruction through the enemy ranks. Each swing of their katanas was a deadly arc, each connection a spray of blood that painted the wet stones beneath their feet. The air was thick with the metallic scent of blood and the acrid smoke from the spreading fire.

Sumiko, with precise and ruthless efficiency, struck down a soldier attempting to regroup and charge. Her blade sliced through the air, finding the gap in his armor and cutting deep into his side. He fell, clutching his wound, as she moved onto her next target without hesitation.

Beside her, Misako fought with a ferocious intensity, her earlier injury forgotten in the heat of battle. She spun and twisted, her katana a blur as she parried an incoming blow and retaliated with a swift thrust through her attacker's throat. The man gurgled and dropped, his eyes wide in shock and pain as he crumpled to the ground.

The sisters' synergy was palpable, their movements synchronized in a deadly dance that left bodies in their wake. Soldiers hesitated as they approached, fear creeping into their hearts as they witnessed the relentless sisters cutting down their comrades with grim determination.

Meanwhile, Aiko, having seized three horses from the now-abandoned stable, mounted one and led the others by a rope. Her silhouette against the blazing fires was like that of a vengeful spirit from the tales of old—a dark angel astride a beast, her katana raised high. She charged through the chaos, her blade singing a song of death as she cut down anyone foolish enough to stand in her path.

Her movements were fluid and precise, each stroke of her katana slicing through the air and cleaving through flesh and bone. Soldiers screamed and fell as she passed, her horse's hooves pounding the cobblestones, splashing through puddles of blood and rainwater. The image of Aiko, a fierce and unstoppable force, was both terrifying and awe-inspiring.

As Aiko neared where her sisters fought, Sumiko and Misako sensed her approach, their hearts lifting at the sight of their sister, not just alive but fighting with the fury of the storm itself. They redoubled their efforts, pushing back against the soldiers with renewed vigor, making their way towards her.

As Aiko, mounted and formidable, approached the fray where her sisters fought desperately against overwhelming odds, the tide began to turn in an almost palpable shift. The moment Sumiko and Misako saw Aiko, not just surviving but thriving as an avenger reborn from her own ashes, their spirits soared. With a gritty determination fueled by sisterly bonds, they fought their way to her, each cut and parry a step closer to reunion.

Sumiko reached Misako first, assisting her onto one of the horses Aiko had brought due to her injured leg, which hampered her mobility but not her fighting spirit. Once mounted, the sisters found their rhythm as cavalry, their movements more coordinated and devastating. Misako, despite her injury, managed to swing her katana with lethal precision, her strikes forceful and decisive.

Together, the three sisters—resembling deities of vengeance straight out of a Japanese saga, perhaps akin to the furious spirits of Yamata no Orochi, the legendary eight-headed serpent slain by the storm god Susanoo—became a storm unto themselves. Their presence on horseback, silhouetted against the flames and chaos of the fortress, cast them as otherworldly beings, demons of retribution riding the tempest of their wrath.

Thunder rolled overhead as if the heavens themselves bore witness to their fury. Each slash and hack from their katanas was met with cries of fear and pain from the soldiers who, now completely overwhelmed by the ferocity and relentless advance of these avenging sisters, began to break ranks in panic. The mythic aura that the Hayashi sisters embodied turned the soldiers' morale to dust; they saw not mere women, but vengeful spirits risen from the lore of their darkest tales.

The fortress, once a stronghold of their torment, became a backdrop to their wrath. Flames engulfed structure after structure, a fire inferno that mirrored the fierce blaze of their united souls. As the sisters pushed through to the exit, they left behind them a trail of bodies and a fortress succumbing to destruction, its defenses as broken as the spirits of the men who manned them.

Riding out of the gates, the sisters did not look back at the chaos they were leaving behind. The fortress, now a blazing hellscape, was a fitting pyre for the horrors they had suffered within its walls. Their faces and armor were splattered with mud and blood, marking them as warriors who had transcended their pain and risen through the fire of vengeance.

The nightmare was no longer theirs but belonged to those who had stood in their way. As they rode into the dimming light of dawn, away from the fortress, the rain began to wash the blood from their armor, symbolic of the cleansing of their past torments. They rode not just as survivors but as triumphant warriors, their bond unbroken, their resolve unyielded, their revenge complete.

•••

8: Dawn of Reunion and Resolve

As the first light of dawn tinted the sky with hues of gold and pink, the Hayashi sisters found refuge by a serene lake, its surface a mirror reflecting the tumultuous journey they had endured. The fortress was behind them now, a fading nightmare swallowed by the distance and the morning mist.

Exhausted, they dismounted near the water's edge, where the sound of the gentle lapping waves offered a stark contrast to the chaos of the night.

Before tending to their wounds or the weariness that clung to their bodies, they sought solace in each other's embrace—a long, unbroken moment where no words were needed.

Misako and Aiko wrapped their arms around Sumiko, their embrace a fortress of warmth and love. Misako, tears streaming down her face, whispered into the quiet morning, "We thought we'd lost you, Aiko. Every day without you was a battle against despair."

Aiko, her own eyes glistening with tears, responded softly, "Every day in that cell, I kept fighting because I knew you wouldn't stop looking for me.

Knowing that kept me alive." Her voice broke as she buried her face in Sumiko's shoulder, her body shaking with the intensity of her emotions.

Sumiko, unable to speak, communicated in the language they all understood perfectly—her touch. She tightened her hold, her hands strong and reassuring on their backs, her eyes moist but shining with an unspoken strength. She then looked at each of her sisters, her eyes conveying a depth of love and relief that words could never capture.

Misako took a deep, shuddering breath, steadying herself against the torrent of emotions. "You're here now. That's all that matters. We're together again," she said, her voice steadying as she pulled back slightly to look at Aiko. "And we're never letting you go again."

They released the embrace only slightly, still holding onto each other, unwilling to let go completely. Sumiko reached up, her fingers tracing the lines of Aiko's face, memorizing the moment, the feel of her sister alive and real under her touch. Then, her hands moved with deliberate grace, signing with emotional depth, I fought for this moment. For us. For our return to each other. Nothing else mattered.

Tears welled in Aiko's eyes as she watched Sumiko's hands, understanding each movement. "I knew it," Aiko murmured, her voice thick with emotion. "I felt it, even in the darkest moments—that you were both out there, fighting for me."

The sisters stood together by the lake, the early morning light encasing them in a soft glow. The world around them was still, save for the gentle sound of the lake's waters lapping against the shore. Here, in this serene moment, the horrors of the past began to recede, pushed away by the overwhelming presence of their united spirits.

As they finally moved to tend to their wounds, their actions were gentle and caring, each touch a reassurance of their presence and their shared future.

The physical care they provided each other mirrored the emotional healing that had begun with their reunion. They were together, they were alive, and they were unbroken.

With their wounds tended, they sat quietly by the lake, watching the sun rise higher, its warmth a gentle balm. Their conversation flowed softly, filled with plans for the future, reflections on their past, and the unspoken promise that whatever came next, they would face it together—as sisters, as survivors, as an unbreakable unit forged through adversity.

•••

As the Hayashi sisters approached their village, the familiarity of the landscape brought a semblance of peace, contrasting starkly with the chaos they had endured. Riding side by side, their horses' hooves kicked up dust on the path that had welcomed them home since childhood. Yet, as they entered, an uneasy silence fell over the gathered villagers. Their eyes flickered with relief at seeing Aiko alive but quickly lowered to avoid direct contact, hinting at troubling news awaiting the sisters.

Puzzled by the atmosphere, which suggested deeper changes during their brief absence, the sister's concern deepened as they drew nearer to their home. There, they were met by the Hakamoto, their father's trusted advisor, his role akin to a deputy responsible for overseeing the samurai's estates in his absence.

The gravity of his bow foretold the weight of his news. "I am sorry to tell you," he began, his voice laden with grief, "but your father is dead. It was an ambush near the bridge at Aizu castle. We were outnumbered, and your father fought like the true samurai he was, a hero until his final breath. He died with honor."

The shock hit the sisters hard, the joy of their reunion crushed under the weight of this devastating news. Misako covered her mouth to stifle a sob, while Sumiko, unable to voice her anguish, expressed her grief through the tightening of her jaw and the clenching of her fists, her eyes blazing with a fierce intensity.

Summoning her resolve, Sumiko communicated through swift, sharp gestures, her signing clear and poignant. Where is his body? Her movements were composed but carried an undercurrent of dread.

The Hakamoto's response was delivered with a profound sorrow. "The enemy took your father's head," he murmured, bowing deeply again. In the samurai culture, taking the head of an enemy was a way to prove victory and, at times, used for posthumous humiliation or ransom. This meant not only the denial of proper funeral rites for their father but also a grave insult to his honor.

This revelation left a heavy silence in its wake. Sumiko signed to Misako, her gestures sharp and resolute. We must avenge him. Misako nodded, her own resolve hardening in the face of their new reality.

The villagers stepped back, giving space to the sisters as they processed their grief and renewed their silent vows for vengeance. The atmosphere was thick with a mixture of respect for the family's sacrifice and a palpable fear of the wrath that might ensue.

As the Hayashi sisters stood together in the village square, united by blood and battle, their expressions were a tapestry of resolve and sorrow. Home at last, they faced not the peace they had longed for, but a new chapter—one demanding courage and vengeance.

Aiko, standing slightly apart, felt a tumult of emotions swirling within her. The news of her father's death, so soon after her own liberation, was a cruel blow. Despite the weeks of torment she had endured, she had clung to the hope of returning to a family made whole.

Now, the reality of their loss gripped her heart with a cold ferocity. Her eyes, which had just begun to rediscover the light of freedom, darkened with the weight of impending duty. As she looked at her sisters, a silent vow passed between them—a vow to honor their father's memory and restore the honor that had been stolen with his life.

The villagers, sensing the gravity of the moment, watched with a mix of awe and fear. The sisters, who had left as daughters of a respected samurai, had returned as warriors forged in the flames of adversity. They were no longer just the bearers of their family's legacy but its avengers, its fierce protectors.

Aiko stepped forward, her resolve strengthening as she joined her sisters. Together, they turned, their backs to the villagers, facing the path that would lead them through this new ordeal. The air around them seemed to pulse with the silent strength of their commitment.

As they walked away, their steps were measured and strong despite the weight of their grief. The villagers parted ways, their whispers fading into a respectful silence. The path before the sisters was shrouded in uncertainty, shadowed by the threat of continued conflict, but they walked it as one— united by a bond that no enemy could sever.

•••

Epilogue

Kasumigaura slept. The villagers, exhausted from days of fear and fire, had begun to believe the worst was over. Aiko was home. The kidnappers were dead. The warriors—Sumiko and Misako—had returned, blood-soaked but victorious.

And yet the night was not at peace.

Inside the Hayashi house, silence lay thick as smoke. The sisters sat around the shrine, each lit only by the soft glow of a candle. No swords. No armor. No father.

Misako's knee bounced with restless energy. Aiko had stopped tending her injuries. Sumiko hadn't moved in hours.

The message had arrived earlier. Delivered by a survivor of the ambush.

Their father had fought to the last. His body lost. His head taken. His swords stolen.

Misako had screamed. Aiko had broken a brush in her hand.

But Sumiko—she had simply stood. As if her bones were turning to steel under the weight.

Now, she signed with sharp, silent gestures. He died with honor. But someone wanted him erased.

Aiko replied, her signs slower. The men who took me... weren't just bandits.

That truth had been gnawing at her since the night of her rescue. The uniforms. The tactics. The silences between their words. These weren't thugs. They were soldiers—or something worse. Controlled. Coordinated. Paid.

Sumiko stood up. Took one last look at the empty altar. Then blew out the candle.

Outside, the wind stirred.

At the edge of the village, a lantern flickered in the dark. A traveler passed—too quiet. Watching the Hayashi house. Listening. Then he turned and vanished into the trees, his footsteps soft, his direction deliberate.

Something had begun.

The fire was gone from the village, but it wasn't over. No. It had only moved—underground. Into whispers, into shadows, into uniforms that didn't match their allegiances.

Kasumigaura had seen war before. But what was coming... was not war.

It was betrayal.

It was silence wrapped in honor.

It was a question none of them were ready to answer.

And deep in the night, three sisters sat awake—mourning a man who died with no grave, clutching only rage, only doubt, only blood.

The first book had closed.

But the next was written in vengeance.

•••

Glossary

Aizu – A powerful domain in northern Japan known for its staunch support of the Tokugawa shogunate during the final years of the Edo period. Renowned for its disciplined samurai and resistance to imperial forces.

Aizu-Wakamatsu – The castle town and seat of power in the Aizu domain. Symbolic of loyalty to the old order and an important setting in the political unrest of late 1867.

Aiko Hayashi – The youngest of the Hayashi sisters. Quietly observant, strategic, and skilled with the bow. Her intelligence and grace are often underestimated by her enemies.

Bakufu – Another term for the shogunate government of Japan, led by the Tokugawa clan during the Edo period. The Bakufu was the military government in place before the Meiji Restoration.

Boshin War – A civil war in Japan (1868–1869) between forces loyal to the Tokugawa shogunate and those seeking to return political power to the Emperor. While the events of

Book One occur shortly before the official start of the war, its tension is a looming presence.

Bushidō – The ethical code of the samurai, emphasizing loyalty, honor, duty, and self-discipline. The Hayashi sisters were trained under these principles.

Commodore Perry – The American naval officer whose arrival in Japan in 1853 forced the country to open its ports to foreign trade, setting off a chain of political and social upheaval.

Daimyō – A feudal lord who ruled over a domain (han) in Edo-period Japan. The Hayashi sisters' father once served under a daimyō from Aizu.

Edo – The former name of Tokyo and the seat of the Tokugawa shogunate. Although distant from the events of Book One, its influence reaches every corner of Japan.

Hayashi, Hiroshi – The father of the Hayashi sisters. Once a respected mid-ranking retainer in Aizu, he chose exile in Kasumigaura, raising his daughters in secret. He upheld the ideals of the samurai even as the country shifted around him. At the end of Book One, he is killed in an ambush near Aizu Castle, and his body is not recovered—only his head was taken.

Hayashi Sisters – Sumiko, Misako, and Aiko, daughters of Hiroshi Hayashi. Trained from childhood in martial arts and strategy. Each possesses distinct strengths: Sumiko is disciplined and silent, Misako fiery and headstrong, Aiko graceful and cunning.

Jigai – A ritual form of female suicide, traditionally performed to preserve honor. Often misunderstood in contrast to seppuku, which was practiced by male samurai.

Kasumigaura – A fictional village in the story, also referred to as the Hayashi village. Remote and peaceful, it is where the sisters were raised and trained by their father. Despite sharing a name with a real place in Japan, this version of Kasumigaura is entirely fictional.

Katana – A traditional Japanese curved sword used by samurai. Misako's preferred weapon.

Misako Hayashi – The middle sister. Bold, emotional, and fearless with the katana. She often charges ahead while others hesitate, driven by a deep sense of justice and pride.

Naginata – A polearm with a curved blade used historically by female warriors (onna-musha) and samurai. Though mentioned occasionally in Book One, it is not Aiko's weapon of choice—her main skill lies with the bow.

Ronin – Masterless samurai who often became mercenaries or outlaws after the fall of their lords. Some enemies the sisters face wear imperial uniforms but act like independent guerilla forces—suggesting they are ronin hired to cause disruption.

Seppuku – Ritual suicide by disembowelment, performed by samurai to preserve honor. Distinguished from jigai, the female counterpart.

Shogun – The military ruler of Japan during the Tokugawa era. The shogun held more power than the emperor in practical terms until the Meiji Restoration.

Shogunate – The military government led by the Tokugawa family during the Edo period (1603–1868). It is the structure the Hayashi family remained loyal to in Book One.

Shōgi – Often called Japanese chess. A strategic game that reflects many of the sisters' tactical training growing up.

Sumiko Hayashi – The eldest sister. Stoic, disciplined, and mute due to a childhood injury. She leads through presence, wielding her weapon and her silence with equal power.

Tessen – A Japanese war fan, sometimes used by samurai for both signaling and self-defense. A minor detail in Book One, it appears as part of the sisters' martial training.

Tōrō – A traditional Japanese lantern often seen in temples and gardens. One appears symbolically near the end of Book One.

Yamato-damashii – "The spirit of old Japan," an ideal of stoic, pure, and disciplined behavior—particularly among warriors. A concept underpinning the sisters' philosophy.

•••

Preview: The Broken Oath

The embers of vengeance have only begun to glow.

After the brutal ambush near Aizu Castle that claimed their father's life, the Hayashi sisters return to Kasumigaura not as daughters—but as warriors forged in blood and fire. Their home may be safe for now, but the world beyond has begun to fracture. Whispers of betrayal reach their ears. Old allies shift like shadows. And behind the scenes, powerful figures are already rewriting the rules of loyalty, duty, and honor.

In The Broken Oath, the second volume in the Daughters of Wars saga, the sisters find themselves pulled deeper into a web of conspiracies that stretches far beyond Aizu. Aiko, recovering from her brutal captivity, discovers that her ordeal was no isolated cruelty—it was a warning. Misako, ever the firebrand, learns that vengeance comes at a price that even she may hesitate to pay. And Sumiko, the silent anchor of them all, must confront the truth about her father's past—and the deadly secrets buried beneath his honor.

As the winds of the Boshin War begin to stir, the Hayashi sisters will uncover a hidden code, a shattered alliance, and an ancient vow once sworn to protect Japan itself. But when oaths are broken and truth is bent, the line between justice and treachery begins to blur.

Enemies close in. Alliances crumble. And from Kyoto to Edo, the storm is building.

The Broken Oath is a tale of espionage, blood politics, and the unrelenting bond between sisters who refuse to kneel—no matter who tries to make them.

The war has not yet begun.
But the betrayal already has.

...

The Broken Oath is out now on Amazon—because peace was never an option, and neither was silence.

Printed in Dunstable, United Kingdom